BLACK WALTZ

BY THE SAME AUTHOR

In Praise of Lies

The Killer

Inferno

BLACK WALTZ

Patrícia Melo

Translated by Clifford E. Landers

BLOOMSBURY

First published in Brazil as *Valsa Negra* by Companhia das Letras, 2003
First published in Great Britain 2004

This paperback edition published 2005

Bloomsbury Publishing Plc, 36 Soho Square, London W1D 3QY

A CIP catalogue record for this book
is available from the British Library

All papers used by Bloomsbury Publishing are natural,
recyclable products made from wood grown in well-managed
forests. The manufacturing processes conform to the
environmental regulations of the country of origin.

ISBN 0 7475 7659 9
9780747576594

10 9 8 7 6 5 4 3 2 1

Typeset by Hewer Text Ltd, Edinburgh
Printed in Great Britain by Clays Ltd, St Ives plc

www.bloomsbury.com/patriciamelo

For J.N.

‘Hate is indistinguishable from love’

Catullus

I

BREAKING BOTH LEGS WOULD be a good solution, I thought, when I met Rachel, my septuagenarian neighbor, returning from the hospital with her leg in a cast. I helped the doorman push the wheelchair into the elevator. It would be great to fall down the stairs and shatter tibias and femurs, stay at home, not have to go to the orchestra and take care of petty crap, not talk on the phone to guys like Felipe Hojas, that exhibitionist bore of a maestro who's always complaining about back pain and canceling concerts right and left, not have to answer the fifty emails that appear every time I turn on the computer, not have that picture of Brahms staring at me like that, not have to conduct in Palermo again, not worry about an accordionist for the Maxwell Davies piece, not look at contracts for spallas, not think for even a minute about Verdi's *Requiem*, the four sacred works, specifically not about that Ave Maria, not go onstage, not get irritated, not scream at the musicians, not rehearse Mahler's Seventh, not do any of that, just stay at home, available, alert, concentrating on Marie.

Rachel asked me to take her to her apartment, on the second floor. I can't spare the time, I thought. Marie had already come out of the bathroom, she was quick; young women don't spend a lot of time on makeup. 'I don't understand how they can put all that crap on their face.

A woman's *nécessaire*, after the age of forty, is a veritable chemical weapons laboratory,' she once said.

We got into the elevator, and as soon as the door closed Rachel took advantage of my presence to complain about 'the stupid people who work in this building', especially 'that scoundrel of a doorman' who had almost broken her other leg as he helped her out of the taxi. She was wound up, Rachel.

'Did you notice it isn't plaster?' she asked, pointing to the plastic structure encasing her leg.

I listened as she explained how, that same morning, as she was walking through the streets of our neighborhood, she'd been swallowed up by a hole. 'Those shitty mayors nowadays only think about the poor. The middle class has been relegated to the back burner. Imagine a hole like that, enormous, right in the middle of the street.'

I have a special talent for imagining holes, all of them very black, deep, whirlpools, and I might have described to Rachel a huge variety of grottoes and caverns, underground openings and fissures, if my desire to say something weren't always engulfed by a profound sense of discouragement. I had been like that lately. At the rehearsal of Mahler's Seventh, the day before, seeing my musicians play lethargically, I felt like telling them that Mahler was no peasant like Bruckner. Bruckner is coitus interruptus, I considered saying. But Mahler is potent in his music, Mahler proposes and executes, develops, delivers. I could have voiced my reservations: you don't rehearse Mahler, you play Mahler, with vigor, respecting the dynamics, or else you just abandon Mahler altogether. That's what I should have said; my musicians would have understood perfectly, would have played better, but instead I lost my temper and shouted at the orchestra and walked out of the rehearsal. Lately I would either get angry or simply remain silent, without the strength to say anything, lacking the will, like now with my neighbor Rachel.

Rachel handed me the key to her apartment, and we went in. I was once again assailed by that smell, a mixture of dust, alcohol, and meat stock. 'I don't smell anything,' Marie would say, when I brought that stench to her attention. But Marie was young and smoked marijuana, and potheads can never smell anything. I could. I've always been an expert on rotten things. If death has an odor, it was this. In the morning, when the residents opened their windows and went out to walk their dogs, when the dying were taken for a sunbath by their nurses, that smell spread throughout the building so pervasively that I had to rub camphor around my nostrils.

The truth is that it hadn't been a good idea for us to move to that apartment. It had been stupid to accept the gift from Henri, my generous father-in-law. 'It has room for your pianos,' he'd said, just after Marie came back from Israel and I left Teresa and our teenage daughter, one hell of a mess. I shoved my pianos in there and before I knew it I was married to Marie. Today I wonder whether that smell of death wasn't the cause of our misfortune. If noisy, primitive music, films full of guns and revenge, can poison our behavior and our fates, if we see all that crap and go out and kill fifteen at McDonald's, why can't smells like that one induce similar acts of insanity? I remember that as soon as we moved to the apartment I asked the neighbors and workers in the building if they noticed the odor. They didn't smell a thing. It's incredible how people have lost the sense of smell.

The stench in Rachel's apartment was even worse, greatly surpassing that of the streets and the lobby. There was also mothballs, which totally nauseated me. Rachel wouldn't let me leave without visiting her late husband's office, filled with dark furniture, junk, knickknacks. Why keep all that crap? 'The water jug,' she shouted. I took the clay piece from a shelf and carried it to the living room. Rachel said she had always wanted to show it to me. 'Isn't it pretty? It's by Eliseo Visconti. He made it for the dressing rooms at the Municipal Theater in Rio.' I listened to a long story about Eliseo and the art form as applied in Brazil, after which I was obliged to view her collection of pre-Columbian art, her eighteenth-century Venetian painting, and the candle-holder that adorned the dinner table – 'it's Sheffield silver before it became silver plate,' she said, as if I had the faintest idea what Sheffield silver or silver plate might be. That's the problem with being a maestro. People are always coming out with that kind of conversation. Nobody talks football with a maestro.

I left the apartment out of sorts, carrying Visconti's water jug as a present. 'It's so useless here,' she'd said, 'it'll look nice in your dressing room.'

It really would be just great to break my legs, I thought as I descended the stairs. To people like Rachel, the lonely, and also for the fucked-over in general, getting sick or suffering an accident of some kind is a way of gaining visibility. My employees at the theater, doormen, cleaning staff, security people, all of them love talking about their visits to the doctor, what the physician had to say about their rotten liver. You may be absolutely nothing, but if you have a rotten liver, at least that's something. You alone have it. It's your rotten liver, your broken leg, your incurable allergy. Falling into that hole was maybe one of the most interesting things that could happen at this stage of Rachel's life. Her small blue eyes seemed even more alive as she pronounced the word *fracture*. She even said that 'breaking my leg didn't hurt at all' and that the orthopedist at Albert Einstein Hospital 'looked just like Robert Redford'.

In my case, however, breaking my legs would be the ideal pretext for implementing my plans regarding Marie. Travel less, cancel the Ottawa and Palermo concerts, not work and stay home, watching my wife, checking, monitoring her movements. Keeping alert and avoiding catastrophe. That's how a real man acts.

I walked to the corner; the streets of Higienópolis were more and more full of dog shit. I got in the car, turned on the radio, searched for a newscast. No news from Israel. They no longer talked about the conflict, it was old news. I waited for less than half an hour and Marie came out of the building. Boots, leather coat, her violin case flung over one shoulder. Who was it that said the devil rides the bow of a violin? There he was, the demon, getting into a taxi. I remembered the day she stuck into my pocket a poem that read more or less: 'I want you, I'm afraid of you, I wait for you, in a word, I'm fucked and radiant, more fucked than radiant, and vice versa.' I was completely excited by that. Deep down, I thought, I exchanged my boring life with Teresa for a handful of uncertainty and anguish at Marie's side. Being with her was having, in one package, both very good and very bad things. More bad than good, to tell the truth.

I got out of the car and went back to our apartment. I'd made up my mind; I wanted to find out once and for all what was going on.

2

'TRIUMPHANT ISRAEL IS A terrible place to drink coffee.' Another page: 'I tell him that the Arabs respect a fat man, a large man can really fuck with their lives.' Page 76, with several exclamation points in the margin: 'Irving Berlin is better than Ariel Sharon.' Another book, same author: 'I am not one of those Jews for whom Christmas is a tremendous provocation.' What was it I wanted from Marie? Why was I once again leafing through the books on her night table, looking for underlined phrases, seeking clues, meanings? The reason for a handful of the underlines was perfectly obvious. Judaism, being Jewish, not being Jewish, bomb-throwing, terrorism, but what about 'the epitome of classical theater'? What made Marie underline such statements? And why would she underline *rich and bloated* and *con games* and *absenteeism*? Why her enthusiastic reading of American writers who never went beyond that boring Judaism-*cum*-sex that I found so irritating? I recalled that, one time in bed, just after we met, she spoke of the color of my hair, black, so black and straight, by then it wasn't all that black, white hairs kept cropping up, and then, after learning that I was a Brazilian Brazilian, the son and grandson of Brazilians, and that somewhere back there was a Portuguese great-grandfather but I didn't rule out a mixture of Indians, Spanish, and blacks, she said something that made me laugh like crazy. 'You're a true subequatorial type,' she said. I laughed a lot about that. A really superequatorial comment, or rather, supraequatorial. Until then we were nothing but similarities. And suddenly I was subequatorial. I sometimes asked myself if Marie would ever forgive me for not being Jewish. Her parents, who at first seemed so flattered by my curiosity about their stories of the diamond trade and business in Antwerp, would surely never accept this slight defect of mine. Not belonging to their world. To their celebrations. Not knowing what Aliyah is. Or Chanukah. Or Galut. Or kike. Shmoock. 'It's pronounced "shmuk",' Marie's mother corrected me when I dared to ask the meaning of the word. A sluggard. A loser. 'Those guys don't have the slightest idea what it is to be Jewish,' in another book, heavily underlined. Those guys. To Marie I was probably included in the 'those guys' category. 'Those guys' were precisely me. 'They don't know anything.' In other words, I was the wrong man. Thirty years older and a goy to boot. A mistake. Maybe Marie felt it would have been better to stay in Tel Aviv, studying violin at the Samuel Rubin Academy of Music with Professor Sandorsky, 'a student of one of Heifetz's favorite disciples', as she liked to refer to the master. To be the student of the disciple is more or less like being the cousin of a cousin. It's eight degrees of separation. It's not even being related; a cousin is superfluous. 'Sandorsky is the famous C-plus,' I'd told Marie. 'Neither very good nor very bad. The one who does it okay.' Marie disagreed. She was constantly defending Sandorsky and spared no praise: 'sensitive', 'disciplinarian', 'a man of genius'. Without doubt it had been Sandorsky who'd uttered the phrase she'd been repeating ever since returning from her trip, that 'she didn't understand how, being Jewish, she could have waited twenty years to go to Israel'.

'Did you have an affair with him?' I once asked.
'Who?'
'Sandorsky.'
'You think I had an affair with Sandorsky?'
'He was crazy about you.'
'Do you always think people are crazy about me?'
'I'm crazy about you.'
'Ricochet effect. I started it all. You merely reacted.'
'But he at least tried.'
'Sandorsky? Poor man. He wouldn't dare.'
'That monkey.'
'You know, there's a name for that.'
'C-plus. That's what he is.'
'Retroactive jealousy. You're jealous of my past.'

A relationship like that doesn't develop by itself. Marie was forever inciting me to that kind of behavior. She liked to inflame me, insinuating, dropping into our conversations, always in a seemingly casual way, names like Jean-Pierre, David, or Henrique, young men with whom she had studied. 'There was nothing between us,' she would tell me, while I burned in hell. She enjoyed doing that to me. I caught on to the game right away. That kind of conversation invariably created great sexual tension between us. We would fight until we got tired and then work everything out in bed. And, after a brief period of peace, the game would start all over again.

At that moment, leafing through the books, I seriously doubted Marie. Women lie, that's the truth. Men deceive, lie and betray, but women deceive, lie and betray even more. Sandorsky didn't strike me as being part of our game. It was something more. It was behind those readings, Marie's recent interest in everything having to do with Israel – bombs, terrorists, peace accords. There was something that definitely united them, something exemplified in phrases like 'Jews in Poland also had terrible enemies. But the fact of having terrible enemies did not mean they could not retain the Jewish soul.' That united them.

If it was music that united them, as it united Clara and Schumann, if Marie, like Clara, was seeking in Sandorsky the knowledge of things like phrasing, progression, dynamics, and meaning, I had a chance of separating them. When music unites two people, in the way Clara was united with Schumann, the way Brahms was united with Schumann, and Clara was united with Brahms, the way Bülow was united with Liszt, and Cosima was united with Bülow, and the way Bülow was united with Wagner, and Wagner was united with Cosima, when music unites two people it's the devil who celebrates the communion. First we love the one who is our musical superior. And later we do everything we can to fuck him.

But it wasn't music that united Marie and Sandorsky, it was their Jewish soul. And about that I could do nothing. Because I was one of those guys who 'don't have the slightest idea what it is to be Jewish'. I knew nothing about the Jews, and even if I learned everything, made every effort – as I had – I still wasn't one of them.

All of this was whirling around in my brain, making me crazy, when I heard the living room door open. It was Jânia, our maid, and she was late. I sat on the bed, disheartened. What harm was there in those books? At Marie's age I too listened to the voice of my masters. But this thought did nothing to make me feel better. Sandorsky must have led Marie on by using the ancient paradigm of the Greek master, who takes you to the truth while he fucks you. A wise old monkey, was Sandorsky. He had become fascinated with the freshness of Marie, her grace, talent and youth. I remember the photos she sent me from Tel Aviv. The two of them embracing in front of the academy, teacher and student, the predator and his victim, Marie wanting to learn about the world and Sandorsky, ravenous, ready to gobble her up. I also remember the enthusiasm with which she had described her classes, soon after arriving in Israel.

'They don't know a thing,' she had underlined in the book. She was talking about me, we don't know anything, we goys, we nothings, we, the maestros, we don't know anything about you. About us. You don't know anything about us. You don't know what it is to be a Jew, don't have the faintest idea of how we've lived and suffered.

I became irritated imagining that all that passion of Marie's for Judaism had more to do with Sandorsky than with the actual fact of Marie being Jewish. Marie, as she herself stated, was part of the 'new Jewish' generation. The Jew who is not first and foremost Jewish, but is also Jewish. The way he's a citizen, the way he's a man, the way he's essentially all things. 'Judaism didn't come first in my upbringing,' she had said.

Thinking these thoughts made me remember the pile of old newspapers underneath our bed. I got down on my knees. There they were, all with headlines like bloody-Sunday-in-Middle-East, violence-and-death-in-Jerusalem, piles and piles of articles that Marie had set aside to read to 'understand Jewish contradictions', but never read and never allowed Jânia to throw out. I picked up a couple of them. More than a hundred injured in a pizzeria. In retaliation, twenty-seven dead. More than eighteen wounded. There was nothing to understand in those newspapers. Just numbers. Killings. Hatred. But Sandorsky wanted to keep her in Israel, smother her with their reality, their bombs. Why didn't he also tell Marie to underline 'Israel has become the most serious threat to the survival of the Jews since the end of World War II'? That they didn't underline. I reached under the bed; I decided to get rid of the papers. I pulled out two piles and took them to the trash. There was another stack of them next to the wall, which I tried to reach with my foot. I had to crawl even further under the bed. A powerful hatred took hold of me, and just as I was pushing the pile of papers, furiously shoving it against the wall, the bedroom door opened suddenly and Jânia came in. I held my breath and followed the sound of her movement around the room.

I closed my eyes, distressed, and, before I could think of some way of getting out from where I was, beneath the bed, Jânia left the room, and as I began to extricate myself, she turned back and caught me in that horrible position. I felt awful, with her looking down at me, and me emerging from that hole like some burrowing animal, some crawling, dust-covered creature. Jânia's expression showed such confusion that I didn't even feel the need to say anything. I muttered some words, 'old newspapers', and she stood there looking at me, the way she always looked when she found me studying in the living room: with a dumb smile plastered on her face.

If, at that moment, I had come out and slammed the door it would have been better, but I managed to make my situation even worse.

'Jânia,' I said, taking her by the arms with a degree of force, 'would you do something for me?' Of course she would. Even before hearing my proposal she was ready for anything. It's amazing how people go along with our offers.

I explained, taking some bills from my wallet, that all she had to do, besides throwing out those newspapers, was to keep an eye on Marie. 'Jot down the name of anyone who comes here,' I said, 'and the people she talks to on the phone.' I also explained that she should listen in on my wife's telephone conversations, using the extension in the kitchen. 'If you don't understand what they're saying, if it's another language, try and see if Marie says Sandorsky.' I made her repeat 'Sandorsky' several times, and she assured me she'd never heard 'anything like that' in the house. 'Do you know how to write?' I asked. I gave her a pen and paper. 'Write "Sandorsky" there.' She didn't do too badly, the awkward handwriting of any semi-illiterate. We now had a deal.

It wasn't yet ten in the morning when I left the apartment. I took some of Marie's books with me. The city was grayer, I wasn't feeling well. I got in the car, looked at the sky. It was going to be a rotten day.

3

'YOU HAVE TO CALL that agent in Switzerland. You have to call Mexico. You have to speak with the coordinator of the orchestra's volunteer services. You have to have lunch with Pedro Ricardo. You have to receive the president of the Foreign Office's cultural service. And you have to talk to the first chair in the double-bass section.' It was necessary to do all that, Adriana, my new assistant, informed me, but first, she emphasized, first I had to rehearse Mahler's Seventh Symphony. I found it funny that Adriana would include the rehearsal in my schedule. As if I didn't know. 'And call Columbia Artists Management Inc.,' without fail, she concluded. She could never say just CAMI; she felt the need to pour out the entire name.

I couldn't complain. Adriana was quite efficient, even if Marie's always saying the opposite. 'She thinks she knows about things. The other day she came to me and said how she loves Haydn's jokes. As if she knew the first thing about music. And she never gives you my messages. When are you going to hire somebody like Dona Ercília or Dona Yollanda, my father's secretaries? And stop laughing, because it's not jealousy. You're mine. I bought you. My problem with the girl is that she's stupid. And incompetent. That's all.'

It wasn't true. Adriana took care of my schedule with great zeal.

As soon as I sat down my cell phone rang.

'Dad?' It was Eduarda, my thirteen-year-old daughter. It had been weeks since I had spoken to her.

'Little Executive?' I asked, looking at my watch. I had given her that nickname right after separating from Teresa. Since then, Eduarda had had a full schedule, ballet, English classes, voice lessons, violin, computer classes, and tennis, with almost no time to attend my concerts or visit me at the orchestra. Actually, that was the way Teresa found to be even more idle. She was all the time nagging me to 'be a father'. To her, 'being a father' meant taking care of the dirty work, whatever she hated doing, picking up, dropping off, buying, and paying. 'I don't have the time,' she would say when she was called upon to accompany Eduarda to friends' parties or to study sessions. 'You go. Why do I have to take care of everything by myself?' I didn't have time either; I was a conductor. I worked like a dog.

'You looked handsome,' Eduarda said.

'Who?'

'You. In the newspaper. That was a cool photo.'

'What photo?'

'Didn't you hear what I said, Dad?'

I was unfocused, and missed a good deal of what my daughter had said. But when I heard the paper had run a story about me I went on full alert. There were lots of things I wanted to talk about with Eduarda, but I was anxious to read the story. 'Call me tonight,' I said, 'I have a rehearsal now.'

I hung up and told Adriana to bring me the newspapers. Anything that came out in the press about me was catalogued by my assistant. We had many folders, an enormous archive filled with reviews, criticism, interviews; one more, I thought, when Adriana gave me the paper. There I was, on the front page of the cultural section, and Eduarda was right, it really was a good photo. I've always been photogenic. Really good, the photo, I thought, at the same time feeling embarrassed at my enthusiasm about such trash. What good was that piece of foolishness? Who even read criticisms, other than my enemies? It was just another opportunity for my detractors to hate me even more. Nothing makes a maestro or musician more infuriated than the success of another maestro or musician. Finding out that so-and-so was invited to conduct some orchestra, or that he won some prize or was praised for a performance – in the musical world such things were like a rabbit punch. We get mad as hell when someone accomplishes anything.

It occurred to me then that Marie could do with stories about me what she did with the articles about Israel. Clip them, keep them, read them with care. It bothered me to think she hadn't even seen me in the paper. I took a few seconds to consider a way of mentioning it. Did you see the article? I could nonchalantly ask before the rehearsal. I felt ridiculous again. As if the article had the power to show Marie my superiority to Sandorsky, the power to make her see that monkey-faced old man as a nobody, a virtual nonentity who devoted himself to the academy because he had never succeeded at anything else. Sandorsky had followed the book to the letter; incapable of creating anything, he had become a know-it-all.

I wanted to stop thinking about all that, imagining that they spoke on the phone every day, were lovers, were Jews, but I couldn't. I felt as if I were stealing something from myself.

I asked Adriana to bring me a Diet Coke with lots of ice. I paced around the room; I needed a few moments before the rehearsal to clear my head, calm down, get into the music, hear my interpretation, hear Mahler, there inside, with substance, pure sound, without thinking about Sandorsky or Marie. I couldn't keep from reopening the book I'd brought from home. Another underlined sentence: 'Let's face it, for Jews the problem is always the goy.' Us goys, we're the problem. She wasn't even worried about the possibility of my opening the book and seeing that underlining; she didn't hide it, she'd underline, and that was that. She didn't exert the slightest effort to make me feel less un-Jewish. And it didn't matter how much falafel I ate or how nice I was at her family gatherings or how famous I was and that I appeared in newspapers. I would never be a Jew. But Sandorsky, well, Sandorsky son-of-the-cousin-of-the-grandson-of-a-disciple-of-Heifetz, he was naturally a Jew. 'He was so large physically; I equated that with masculinity' – another underline. I closed the book. Definitely, I would not come under the heading 'height'. I wasn't tall. I put the book back in the drawer. I was short. Marie smiled from the picture frame, in Tel Aviv. I turned it to the wall.

I tried to concentrate on Adriana's appointment book. Meeting with the head of the double-bass section, three o'clock. I already knew what he wanted. 'We prefer the German school,' Hamilton had said, after the last rehearsal. As if the way you hold the bow mattered, as if it changed anything. I felt like suggesting a different guideline for our meeting, none of this German school or French school, what if we talk about the playing-well school? Playing well every day. Rehearsing for long periods. Working. Not missing notes in rehearsals. Memorizing the scores. Lunch with Pedro Ricardo, one o'clock.

'I'm like you, I love this garbage,' Adriana said, coming back into the room carrying two cans of Diet Coca-Cola on a tray.

'Who's this Pedro Ricardo?' I asked.

'Mr. Spontaneous,' she replied. 'He wants to organize a football team for the orchestra. I'll tell you how spontaneous people work. They open the newspaper, read an article about our orchestra and show up here, offering things, encyclopedias, surgical gloves, dental care, computer stands, anything you can imagine. That's what happens if you're successful. I wonder if they offer soccer coaches to the Rio Philharmonic.'

'Is he the one from Corinthians?'

'The same. You spoke to him last week. Poor guy. His team got fucked on Sunday.'

'Did you see the game?'

'I'm a São Paulo fan.'

So was I. We spoke about the new winger, a real bungler. How could he have missed that goal? Now we had to win the next game to make the play-offs. The truth is that Adriana calmed me with her ability to listen and her sense of humor. A good-humored woman is almost everything. And pretty. Pretty eyes. 'I don't even take it into consideration,' my ex-wife used to say, 'when you praise newcomers to the orchestra. It's just the first stage; later you come to detest them. You intensely love novelties in order to hate them more intensely afterwards.' It wasn't good to think of Teresa at that moment. You live with a woman for thirty years, and when it's over that's all there is? To say that, in that way, in front of our daughter – to say that, for me, love was merely preparation for fresh hatred? Just a pretext to ruin and destroy? 'You're selfish. You're only concerned about yourself, and nothing else. Me-me-me. It's no accident you're a conductor. There's no one more self-centered than a conductor. You're practically autistic. Nothing matters to you.' 'Your hatred machine,' she had said. Your 'private shredder'. Teresa was like that now, she would say things. During all the years we were together, Teresa would use a sensational technique to put me down. Suddenly, with no explanation, in the midst of nothing, at dinner, on an ordinary morning, or after one of my presentations, in the dressing room as I was being congratulated by friends, without anything abnormal having happened to justify her behavior, she would give me the silent treatment. It wasn't just any silence, it was a silence that shot from her eyes like poisoned arrows, an extremely potent weapon that Teresa used to leave me on the outside, to exclude me from my own success, from my center. And it worked. As soon as she shut down, I would feel a morbid need to implore and be accepted, I wanted to please her, amuse her. The worst thing was that her taciturnity generated a contagious sense of malaise, which began with me and spread out, into the people around us, and suddenly a powerful atmosphere of constraint was created. I hated that, especially because, try as I might, I was unable to assert my logorrhea; there was silence, the absence of Teresa. But now, after I had abandoned her to live with a girl five years older than our daughter, Teresa had renounced her pathological silence, adopted another method, one of words that kill. Saying everything. Saying horrible things.

'There are days when I'm that way myself,' said Adriana, pouring more Coke into my glass.

I pretended not to understand her remark. I hate that type of talk-therapy. I went into the bathroom, looked in the mirror; my face was absolutely normal. What was Adriana talking about anyway? My face was expressionless. When it comes to impenetrability, I know of few people better than I. I simply close the door and turn my back. I returned to the room and went on drinking, silently.

'I know you were once an alcoholic,' she insisted.

'You do?' I asked.

'From day one.' Pause. She showed me the can of Coke. 'Nobody but former alcoholics like you and me drink this crap with such gusto.'

I really did drink a lot of Coke. Every day, before and after rehearsal. And Adriana knew how to make it the way I liked, with lime and a lot of ice. But I was never an alcoholic, although I didn't tell her that. Nor did I ask anything. It was time for the rehearsal.

Before I reached the door, she stood in front of me, a comb in her hand. She was wearing a cut-off T-shirt, I could see her pierced navel. Very sexy. She fixed my hair, commenting that she'd never known a conductor with hair as unruly as mine. 'I'm going to introduce you to Muti.'

It was good to have Adriana with me. I was taking a liking to her. An ex-alcoholic with a dimple in her chin and knowledgeable about football. Not a good combination.

4

I AVOIDED LOOKING AT Marie at the start of the rehearsal. Actually, I only looked at her in the third movement of the symphony, and what I observed in no way reminded me of the girl I had met a year before, auditioning for the orchestra, playing a Wieniawski concerto with such passion and femininity, as if the violin were part of her, an extension of her own body. Nothing in her music, in her way of playing, caught my attention. I merely noticed that she wasn't wearing a bra. And that her breasts moved back and forth, in time to the notes, exuberantly firm. And that her blouse, which displayed an attractive neckline, was of an almost transparent fabric. The man sharing her music stand, a long-haired would-be soloist, a low-class type who was all the time referring to Bach and Beethoven as 'the dude', could barely turn the pages of the part, so absorbed was he in Marie's beauty. I totally lost my concentration.

It happened in the symphony's third movement, where there was a technically complicated coda, sudden changes of tempo which demand great attention on the part of the conductor, the musicians, and especially the strings. Marie and the frustrated longhair ruined everything. The two of them seemed to misread the notes and, even worse, played without me, not looking at me. I stopped the rehearsal, with the horrible feeling that something was vanishing, as if I were losing the tenuous line that goes beyond music, as if there were no continuity in Mahler's work.

'It's me you must look at,' I said.

We started over, and it was a disaster. Marie got lost again, played several wrong notes, always without looking at me, focusing only on her music stand. I stopped the rehearsal once again, shouting this time, throwing my baton to the floor.

'It's not possible, Marie, in this passage, for you to look at the part. It's me you must look at. Look at my goddamn baton. You have to know this passage by heart. It's the only passage you have to know by heart.'

Marie stood up.

'Sit down!' I shouted.

I didn't look at her again. I forged ahead, conducting in a rage. I ignored her indignant air, her feeling of humiliation, the loss of tempo, the erratic rhythm.

I ended the rehearsal by telling the musicians that I knew of few orchestras in the world capable of dismembering Mahler that way, and that I felt like canceling the concert. I saw that Marie was crying as I descended from the stage, with the violinist practically kneeling at her feet, consoling her. Nothing unites an orchestra more than a good tongue-lashing. They play each against the other whenever they can, but if somebody receives a dressing-down, they all suffer in perfect synchrony. Perhaps an orchestra is in fact only cohesive and organic at the moment they share hatred for the conductor. Suddenly, impelled by rancor, all the sections start to behave like the brass, they relax, take on a certain humanity, become sensitive to the other's suffering, and they unite. Against the conductor.

I passed by my assistant, and asked her to phone Hannah,

in Switzerland. Marie came into the room at the moment when the connection was being made. Generally I limit myself to five minutes when I talk to agents; I don't waste time on gigolos. All I had to do was to tell Hannah it was August and we still didn't know who would be playing the roles of Erda and Fafner and that she needed to work faster. But I drew out the conversation, I spoke of Hojas, the Mexican conductor, 'a sonofabitch who wants me to change the entire routine of the orchestra just because he has a concert in Mexico and would like to come late.' 'Here I am thinking whether he'd ask something like that of the Chicago orchestra,' she replied. We laughed. We laughed, but I didn't like it. What she'd said irritated me. I asked Hannah to give me some details about the crazy who'd entered Parliament in the canton of Zug, killing fourteen people and wounding eighty. It did no good for her to say that the tragedy had gained international attention because the murder of a politician was something 'extremely rare' in Switzerland. 'I'm forty-five,' she said, 'and I've never seen an incident like this.' 'When the Swiss kill, it's wholesale,' I rejoined. Now it was her turn not to like the jokes we were making. ' "A Chamber Drenched in Blood" is the headline in our leading newspaper,' I insisted. Hannah had irritated me for some time. She once told me that she would just love to see Rio's shantytowns. She didn't want to visit our beaches, our forests. She wanted to see our poverty. See our fucked-over, our rot, in the same way she probably enthused over Iraqi films at festivals in Geneva. A real idiot. With hairy armpits. 'You Swiss are on the front page of all the newspapers here,' I said before hanging up.

I pretended not to notice Marie pacing around the room like a hungry tiger. The more she fumed before my eyes, the calmer I acted. As soon as I hung up the phone, she accused me of being tyrannical, coarse, and cruel, in that order. She had to wait for my call to Mexico to say the rest. I explained to Hojas that he couldn't arrive late. 'I don't know how it is there in Mexico, but here in Brazil we don't postpone our rehearsals. We're systematic.' It's surprising the ability people have not to surprise us. The Mexican simply did what I had imagined, and canceled the concert. 'I'm very sorry,' he said. Those sons of bitches do that, cancel concerts. Guest conductors are all a bunch of faggots, with as many demands as if they were stars.

I hung up the phone, and we began round two. Marie said I couldn't yell at her in front of the musicians. So rude. So authoritarian. So disrespectful. She also said that I was being unfair.

'What do you suppose the musicians think when you do that do me?'

'They think you're playing badly.'

Marie went on being audacious, saying that she hadn't missed any notes. OK, maybe a few. But, after all, it was only our first rehearsal.

'So what?'

'Rodrigo sits to the inside of the stand.'

'I don't imagine it's easy for Mr. Longhair to turn the page for his partner, and it's probably not because of the feeling of inferiority that it evokes. I don't think he minds being your slave.'

'What are you talking about?'

'About slavery.'

I noticed how that disconcerted Marie, but I was simply unable to stop. I wanted Marie to fuck herself, for her to have nothing other than me, not music, or money, or the violin, or Sandorsky, nothing. And for her not to wear that exhibitionist blouse. Since I couldn't say that to her, I said other things, also horrible. I spoke of her lack of rhythmic precision, the bowing that disagreed with the rest of the section, the careless dynamics, the discarded ends of phrases, the ill-prepared and technically flawed passage. I was really very good at that, I knew how to destroy a musician. I knew all the terms, the technique, all I had to do was start the engine and run over them.

Marie was no longer as furious; now she was just a 'thing' crumbling, falling, crying, and I pressed ahead. When she said that the entire string section was hurt by what I'd said, I became more wound up than ever. 'Oh really? The middle class of the orchestra feels offended? Because it loses the pacing? Because it doesn't know its goddamn part?'

It broke my heart to see my wife so fragile, sobbing, I felt like hugging her and asking her forgiveness, but before I realized it, I was adding to the damage, 'Yes,' I said, 'I'm not easy, I'm intolerant, I yell at the musicians, I demand obedience and discipline, and I imagine that your section, professional sufferers that you are, considers my attitude inexcusable. You think you already suffer enough, isn't that right? You study a lot, and you're all the time getting bawled out because you never manage to sound like a group. Know what I expect of your friends who aren't happy with me? That they go fuck themselves. That they resign. That they go look for some nice little conductor. As for you, make use of your afternoon off and study. Practice scales and arpeggios.'

Marie was already terribly offended, but I wanted to hurt her even more. It wasn't hard to find the final insult.

'And put on some less provocative clothes for rehearsal,' I said. 'That way, maybe Rodrigo can manage to turn the pages.'

Marie's transformation was impressive. She looked at me

for a few seconds, incredulous, disappointed, and then began to laugh, although she found nothing funny. She left the room without saying goodbye.

Why was I turning my back on myself, allying myself against me, acting as my own enemy? What was my me-against-myself doing, ultimately? Asking Marie to leave me? Go after her and do something, I thought. Make her come back. Even if by force. Run. It took me some three minutes to obey myself.

Marie was on the pedestrian island on Eça de Queirós Avenue, trying to make it across. The chaotic city traffic disoriented me. I didn't know what to say. 'Marie,' I shouted.

She ignored me. I ran to her side, dodging the vehicles speeding past. She didn't let me speak. She hit me in the chest. 'Get out of my life. Now.'

I thought about saying something good for both of us, something to unite us, but I don't know what happened, the noise dazed me, and I could feel nothing but more rage. 'What do you have to tell me about Sandorsky?'

'What are you talking about?'

'I'm talking about Sandorsky.'

'What does that have to do with the two of us?'

'There's nothing superior about being Jewish,' I said, quoting Roth or another of those authors whose books she was always reading.

Marie stood there looking at me, startled, as if she and Sandorsky hadn't underlined that very sentence. As if that sentence didn't mean exactly the opposite. As if there weren't underlinings everywhere. Books and more books. As if Jews weren't famous for excluding others. As if she hadn't destroyed my concentration during the rehearsal. As if there were no newspapers piled under our bed.

The cars buzzed around us.

'I don't know what you're talking about.'

'I'm talking about bombs exploding in Israel. Why don't you pack your bags and go back there?' I continued.

Marie crossed the street in a run. I stood there in the middle of the avenue, the cars and motorcycles, the world around me, making an infernal racket.

5

'MY TENNIS WENT BUST,' Eduarda said on the phone.

'You want money for more lessons?' I asked, opening my wallet and thinking I'd have to stop at an ATM.

My daughter explained that wasn't what she meant. My-tennis-went-bust meant that her tennis game had been canceled. And that she was available that night, we could get a pizza. Or go to the movies to see a 'really cool' film whose name she couldn't remember.

'I'm in a meeting, I'll call you in two minutes,' I said.

I dumped ice into a glass and had a Coca-Cola. I was finally at peace. Over the years, I had developed a rather efficient method for achieving a degree of tranquility. Working myself to death, that was my technique. Burying myself in the orchestra, solving every problem, talking on the telephone, fund-raising, shouting, signing contracts, firing people, putting together a football team, having as my routine a frantic state of agitation, as if I depended on that dynamic to keep my head above water. I felt like a blender grinding up food. An airplane in the sky. A whirling propeller. At the end of the day, I would reach that stage in which exhaustion and peace are almost the same thing. That's why I was there, sprawled on the sofa, without the slightest desire to go home and face Marie. Fighting with Marie was as wearying as making up with her, and at that moment I didn't have the strength for either. I just wanted to watch wrestling on television and not think about anything. But there was no peace with Marie.

The truth is that you can't think about peace when you marry a woman thirty years younger. There's always a great deal of danger surrounding that type of relationship; any thirty-year-old man can be a threat, any trip to work, any girlfriend with ideas, any novelty, any change – everything brings risks with it, and there is also time, the great enemy. Waking up and seeing your face in the mirror, as wrinkled as the pillowcase, being constantly enchanted by the vitality of your mate, isn't a good thing. Especially when we act like one of those Shakespearean characters whose every third thought is about their tomb. It's like that with me. I think about the end every day, my end, the end of everything. Even when I get a massage I can't stop thinking that in fifty minutes that nice sensation, that feeling of well-being, will be over. Some time ago, I stopped getting massages. My preoccupation with the end is so strong that I can barely relax. It was no different with Marie. I could never relax in relation to the two of us. As soon as we started fucking, I knew that it would come to an end, and sooner than everything else, because Marie was too good. Too pretty. Too talented. And, especially, too young. I don't know whether she would have overlooked my age if I weren't a conductor. If I were a trumpet or trombone player. At first, when female musicians come into the orchestra, long before deciding whether they'll be in the part that wants to hate or the part that wants to love the maestro, when they hope to gain status and the other musicians' trust, they're enthusiastic about everything, about our moodiness, our authoritarianism, our narcissism. Once the enchantment passes, however, they accuse us of being moody, authoritarian, and narcissistic.

'Promise me you'll never go to bed with another woman,' Marie said.

'The shop's closed,' I would answer.

'No woman at all.'

'I promise.'

'Put a plaque on your forehead: "Under new management".'

' "Sold," that's what I'm going to put. "Notice: give up".'

These heated dialogues still took place, but more and more I had the impression that they were part of a quota, a slice of happiness, and that it was going to end, and that the only way of not thinking about it was to dedicate myself furiously to the orchestra. That was how I escaped myself. I had worked hard that day. I'd even set up a football league. 'We've had quite good results with bringing people together in businesses,' said the coach, who defined himself as 'a guy who loves a show, loves music of every kind, including what you play here.' He assured me we would create a friendly atmosphere in my 'band'. A climate of friendliness, camaraderie. I laughed when I recalled our conversation. 'You don't need to believe in the musicians. It's enough to believe in football,' he said. Camaraderie. That's a laugh. The man didn't understand the first thing about musicians. In the artistic world, nothing is more poisonous than the musical universe. I remember a writer friend telling me that, until he became a melomaniac, he considered the literary scene the most defamatory in the artistic world. 'But you people,' he said, 'call each other scumbags, lowlifes, and faggots. We don't do that. When we want to bad-mouth a writer, we say we haven't read his latest book. We're reticent. We say, "So-and-so writes well," just like that, very laconically, which signifies in plain English that we hate that writer. But we never say that the guy's a piece of crap. You people come down hard, mercilessly. You're worse than us. Even worse than theater actors.' And that coach was wanting to save us through football. Poor guy.

'I want to be the goalie,' I'd told the coach, accepting his offer. Now that I was a bit empty, semi-anesthetized by fatigue, the idea didn't seem so bad. It might work out.

There was no one else in the theater except two security guards patrolling the halls and Adriana, typing at her noisy keyboard. I thought it would be a good idea to have a pizza with Eduarda. I wouldn't go home, I decided. Maybe I'd sleep at a hotel. What could I say to Marie? I turned on the TV in my room. The number of dead in the new Intifada had risen to 700 Palestinians and 177 Israelis. That's what the newscast said. Maybe I should call Marie and tell her. Suggest she go to Israel to witness the collapse of the peace talks in person.

I phoned Eduarda and told her to wait for me at the entrance. Just after we separated, Teresa had persuaded me to continue having dinner at their house at least once a week. It didn't take long for me to realize the purpose of those get-togethers. 'Did you see the interview with Lebrecht?' she had asked one of the last times we saw each other. Of course I hadn't read it. I don't like prophets of the apocalypse of classical music. Teresa knew that. But she no longer cared about my opinions. She had completely switched sides. I should read Lebrecht, she'd said. Without fail. Because, after all, Lebrecht was one of the 'few thinkers in classical music. He destroys all of you. He gives conductors an incredible lambasting. Says you're a kind of artificially manufactured hero with a nonmusical purpose.' To her, Lebrecht was quite reasonable. 'After all, conductors, not you, of course, but conductors in general, aren't artists anymore. I mean, creators. Who among our maestro friends still composes? Almost no one. They're all mediocre technicians. The fact is that in Brazil there aren't any maestros. All we have are some pretentious types who flail their hands in front of musicians.' It was one thing, in Teresa's opinion, to be a maestro, another, completely different, to be a composer. 'To create important works.' I was amazed at the nonchalance with which she said all those things, as if I weren't a maestro. Or, worse yet, as if I couldn't be a composer, which was true. And all of it in Eduarda's presence. That killed me. But I was also floored in other situations, when everything went well, when Teresa left music aside and talked about domestic issues, burst pipes, dishonest cleaning ladies, taxes, bank statements, contracts, and other real-world drivel, as if our boring past life had flowed without problems, as if we weren't sinking. All of it was horrible. It was horrible in any shape or form. There was no reason to persist with those destructive we're-going-to-keep-the-family-together sessions. There was nothing left to be saved. Only Eduarda. I confess I felt little pleasure in picking her up after school, taking her to the movies, listening to her long, disjointed stories. I was incapable of establishing a dialogue with my daughter, never getting beyond that silly how's-school, been-to-many-parties, how-about-your-English-test? I blamed myself for looking upon those activities as fatherly obligations, and I sometimes begged Marie to go with us.

That night, Adriana accompanied us. Actually, she got into my car and asked for a ride, just as I was leaving the garage of the orchestra building. And she ended up going to get Eduarda with me. She went with us to the pizzeria, which featured pizzas of unimaginable flavors, such as guava paste with cheese, cream of passionfruit, banana pizza, frankfurter pizza, things like that. 'In reality,' Adriana said, 'pizza's no longer a dish, it's a conveyer. A vehicle for transporting any other food, sweet or savory.' That pizzeria was proof of it. Later, Adriana dragged us to a shopping center, saying she knew of a 'fantastic cosmetics store'. She and Eduarda amused themselves buying glitter, lipstick, and nail polish, then they dragged me to a stationery store and picked out writing paper and stickers. We also went to a music store, where Eduarda spent her allowance on a pile of crap. All I had to do was follow the two of them, agree with everything they said. But as fatigue mounted, my mood changed. I became less hollow, more unsure, and then it happened. I was overcome by a terrifying sense of repentance about Marie. Why had I mistreated her so at the last rehearsal? Marie loved me, had given up everything because of me, her studies, she'd come back from Israel, and here was me making a scene, throwing my baton on the floor and yelling at her in front of the orchestra. Even worse, paying Jânia to spy on her, why had I done that? Why suspect Sandorsky, or rummage through her books? What was the importance of sentences like 'Inside every Jew is a multitude of Jews'? They were just phrases, phrases about Jews. It was natural for Marie to seek her identity. Why look for extra meanings behind those underlined sentences? Why create a chasm between us? Suddenly, while Adriana and Eduarda tried on everything they saw in the store windows and asked my opinion, I felt totally lucid. The books were nothing more than that, underlined paragraphs. And what was the problem with a transparent blouse? After all, it wasn't actually all that transparent. I decided to go home immediately. It was also at that moment that I realized that the whole world was blocking my exit. It's hard to escape from a shopping center. And if you're with two women, practically impossible. They fool you, they stop in every store, they drag their feet. And there's no way out, or there are many ways out, the crowds, the lines, the cars, everything blocks your path. I speeded, ran traffic lights, honked, called Marie on my cell phone repeatedly, compulsively, and she didn't answer.

I took an extremely complicated route to drop off Adriana. Then Eduarda. And when I finally got home, the doorman put his two cents in. He asked me to take a package from the pharmacy to Rachel's apartment. 'I'm by myself here at the desk,' he said. Sometimes life is only that, one obstacle after another. Maybe that was why I wasn't able to compose. No sooner had I woken, than reality would begin eating away at me. The orchestra, the musicians, bureaucracy, facts. And now Rachel. I rang the bell and she opened the door, in her wheelchair, talking to her daughter Esther on the cordless phone. I waited for her to finish and listened to her complaints. She was feeling lonely, in pain from the fracture, and her daughter thought only of the stock market. It hurt me tremendously to see Rachel crying, depressed.

'Why do our children hate us?' she asked, as if I were part of Esther's brotherhood.

'Have you eaten anything?' I asked.

She had ordered a pizza. Her maid hadn't shown up that day, and the sour smell in the house was even worse. 'Will you help me to the bedroom?'

It was easy to lift her from the wheelchair to the bed. Rachel was as light as a child. I placed her there and arranged the pillows. Then I got her a glass of water from the kitchen. 'Do you think calling your own daughter and asking for a little attention is being melodramatic?'

'It depends,' I said. I didn't like to get into family arguments. 'Take your medicine.'

'Do you like your mother?'

'Take your medicine.'

I adored my mother. After she died, for many years I had the sensation that I had forgotten to do something, before going to bed. It was to phone her, as I used to do every night. To tell her Teresa and Eduarda were all right, that the concert had gone well, to recount the news. There wasn't a single day that I went to bed without speaking with her.

'She hasn't even seen my cast, the x-rays, nothing,' Rachel said. 'All she wanted to know was whether I had gotten the receipts for reimbursement.'

Before I left, I asked if she was going to be OK.

'I'll be like I always am,' she said.

I knew Marie was at home as soon as I got out of the elevator. The place reeked of marijuana. I knocked on the bedroom door; the TV was tuned to CNN.

'Marie, open this door.'

I could hear a report on the fifty years of visceral enmity between Palestinians and Israelis as I tried to convince Marie to open the door. There was no way. I remembered having seen a hammer around the house and began searching through the closets. In the kitchen I found a meat mallet. I never knew how easy it was to break down a door; two, three blows are more than enough.

Marie was in bed, wearing a T-shirt and panties, with a lamp in her hand, as if that could threaten me.

I sat beside her and said something along the lines of you-want-to-be-a-good-violinist, but Marie didn't let me finish.

'I have just one thing to say to you: go fuck yourself. You think I need your orchestra? That I have to submit myself to your authoritarianism? Who do you think you are?'

'There, I'm the conductor.'

'You can't humiliate me in front of the musicians. I'm your wife.'

'In the orchestra you're a violinist. You have to play well.'

'What happened there has nothing to do with playing well. "And put on some decent clothes to rehearse." That's what you told me. I'm not some yes girl. I do as I like. I wear what I want to. You don't own me.'

'You own me. You're everything to me. I don't want anyone else to see those breasts.'

She was enjoying it now.

'Everything there is mine,' I said, turning off the television. 'The breasts, that wonderful ass, that wet pussy that I love to lick. You're not going to show anything. To anybody.'

Marie got up, setting down the lamp.

'You should stop smoking marijuana,' I said, trying again to hug her.

'Go away.'

'I love you.'

'Cynic.'

'Marijuana and violins don't mix.'

'Idiot.'

Marie punched me in the chest. I grabbed her wrists, forcibly, and she began kicking me.

'Forgive me,' I whispered in her ear.

'Never,' she said, kneeing and kicking me. I saw nothing, and pushed Marie to the bed, struggling with her clothes, Marie cursing me, kicking me, I licked her muscles, her chest, she grabbed my hair, I moved downward, she scratched my face, I bit her waist, she pounded on my back, I licked her groin. In no hurry now, I covered her adolescent thighs with kisses, and only then did I devour her sex, hungrily.

I don't remember the exact moment Marie stopped hitting me. The rest of the night was very good.

6

I AWOKE AT FIVE, totally sleepless, the taste of blood in my mouth. In the bathroom mirror I saw a cut on my lower lip from a bite by Marie. I returned to the bedroom laughing; I always ended up looking like a dog trainer after a night like that.

I jumped back in bed, turned on by seeing Marie's body, asleep and clutching the pillow. I kissed her arms, licked her neck, forgetting my promise to let her sleep late. 'Maniac,' she said as I removed her panties. It was so good to fuck Marie!

Before making love, there was what she called the 'long session'. 'I like foreplay,' she would say, 'kissing', 'kiss me, give me your tongue', and I would go crazy just from hearing her accelerated breathing, or feeling her muscular legs wrapped around my back. After orgasm, I was overcome by a sensation of completeness, of subjection, the world can fuck itself, I thought, all I want is this woman and nothing else. I remember that before I separated from Teresa, Marie and I would make plans that included children and a quiet life in the country, where I would finally dedicate myself to composing. All this seemed wonderful to me because, with the exception of our sexual rapture, our happiness had a certain artificiality to it, which made me feel like the pilot of an aircraft; it was enough to fly, and to go on autopilot whenever it was opportune. It was very comforting to think that I was the pilot, perhaps in the beginning I really was, but later things changed and I lost the sense of control, lost the certainties, and it was in that state of confusion that I abandoned everything and married Marie.

At first I was afraid of what would happen to our life of waking up and fucking, rehearsing and fucking, studying and fucking, always together, all the time, fucking or working. It can't end well, I used to think. Up till then I had always taken seriously Bernstein's commandment, 'Don't fuck the band'. A pretty woman is always a danger. She comes into your orchestra and immediately sets the musicians on fire, all of them wanting to screw the new harpist, the new violinist, the new flutist. It's impossible to compete with the trombonist for a woman and still exercise leadership over the musicians.

So I had never had a relationship with a musician who worked with me. I had never fallen into that trap. It was Marie, with her musicality, her dazzling intelligence, and her typically Jewish beauty, who led me to violate rule number one for any maestro who wants to avoid headaches. Her absolute power over me made me feel impervious to other women. 'Now I'm a limp-dick,' I told Marie, and it wasn't a lie. I had in fact become free from women.

In the beginning, everything was motivating, instigating. But an orchestra is an entity united against the conductor, and Marie quickly felt shunned by her friends, who considered her a spy. 'Being the conductor's wife,' she would say, 'is worse than being the concertmaster. The concertmaster, just like me, is the bridge between the conductor and the orchestra, except that he knows he can't get too friendly with the conductor because then he becomes a doormat, and he can't get too friendly with the musicians because then he becomes a corporatist. He's aware of this and acts in such a way as to exert authority without being insolent. He can be friends to both the musicians and the conductor, if he's careful. He can be an enemy too. Of the musicians. Or of the conductor. But there are options. He has ways of dealing with it. Not me. I'm your wife, and that's that. Even before being a violinist, I'm your wife. If they're talking and I come up to them, everyone shuts up. They don't invite me to anything because they hate me for being your wife, or because they don't want you to think they're sucking up to you.' Marie therefore felt very sensitive about my comments. Once, for example, during a rehearsal, I caught her yawning. I immediately interrupted the orchestra. 'One moment, ladies and gentlemen, Marie has something important to tell us.' She became disconcerted, and the musicians laughed at the situation. When we left after the rehearsal, the roof almost caved in. 'I already have to put up with pressure from the musicians, and on top of that you ridicule me in front of them?' I explained it was just a joke, that Eleazar used to do it with his musicians, and that was what was funny about it, which is why we all laughed. Marie went on pressing me, and then I got irritated too, and told her that her yawning offended me. 'You want to yawn, yawn at some Godard film, not at my rehearsals.' OK, I wasn't an easy person either. We fought a lot because of all these things, there were many misunderstandings, many possessive feelings on my part, much suspicion, demands. But invariably our tension would dissolve in bed.

That day, lying with Marie's body intertwined with mine, I was overtaken by a tremendous sense of well-being and tranquility. I thought we'd have a pleasant Saturday, spending a good part of the day there, fucking. I thought about *Nights in a Spanish Garden*, for piano and orchestra; I had to start preparing the concerts for Naples and Trieste. I thought about what Cláudio, my assistant, had said recently about the fact that I conduct from memory and that he didn't feel confident about doing the same. I thought that conducting from memory had nothing to do with confidence and that I was probably less self-confident than Cláudio. I thought Cláudio would be returning to Toronto in two weeks. And that Marie and I would have lunch in my favorite restaurant, where I would order green pasta. I thought I should choose a special restaurant for the Finnish maestro who was in charge of that evening's concert. Then I thought I shouldn't waste time worrying about a good place to take him, since what foreigners really like is barbecue. I thought that I was afraid to eat meat in Europe because of mad cow disease. I thought that, in our house, the only one who ate meat every day was Jânia. I thought that Jânia was a carnivore. And I leapt out of bed.

Remembering our maid ruined my peace of mind. She'll be getting here soon, and she'll destroy everything, I thought. What had possessed me to offer Jânia money to spy on Marie? A severe character flaw. I was a real sonofabitch. The words that came to mind were horrible.

I got up carefully so as not to wake Marie. I would speak to Jânia and clear everything up.

'Jânia,' I said as soon as she opened the door, 'I want to explain something to you.'

Jânia didn't let me speak; she immediately began saying that a man had called but she didn't remember his name. I replied that I was no longer interested and that it wasn't necessary for her to tell me anything.

'But you were right,' Jânia insisted.

'Stop listening behind doors,' I said, in an almost aggressive tone.

'He said you were coarse.'

'I don't want to know,' I replied, controlling my aggression.

'He called you all sorts of names.'

Stop, I said. Or rather, thought. Stop. I don't want to know. Who had said those things?

'He plays in your group.'

'Fine. I don't want to know.' It was Rodrigo, the frustrated longhair. I didn't want her to tell me anything more. 'All you have to do,' I explained, 'is tell Marie, as soon as she wakes up, that you decided to clean our bedroom and throw out the old newspapers.'

Jânia looked at me, smiling.

'Say it: I threw out the old newspapers. By mistake.'

'She's going to be mad at me.'

I explained that she wouldn't have to return the money I'd given her the day before, although she was being relieved of her duty. I was so ceremonious that Jânia didn't understand a thing. 'Are you firing me?'

I repeated the explanation in less euphemistic terms, leaving it clear that she was still employed and that all she had to do was tell Marie it had been her idea to throw out the papers. Not mine.

'But it *was* yours. You threw everything in the trash. She's going to yell at me.'

'Jânia,' I shouted. She was startled. I lowered my voice. 'Jânia, you only have to say you didn't know anything. You didn't know she wanted to save the newspapers. That's all.'

'But I did know,' Jânia said. 'She always tells me not to throw out the papers.'

Only then did I understand the situation. Jânia had understood everything, right from the start. I reached for my wallet and took out some money. 'So then, we're agreed. You say you didn't know, and that's it.'

Jânia agreed, solicitously.

'And don't forget,' I said. 'I don't want to know anything.'

I thought about asking the name of the person who had phoned, but what for? It's been mentioned already that an orchestra is divided into three groups: those who love you, those who hate you, and those who don't care what you do. You should only care about these last ones, for they're the ones who do everything you say. Maybe my orchestra was different; much less than a third loved me, unless they were faking it. And surely there were well over a third who hated me. It would be more accurate to divide them into two parts: half hated me and half didn't care. Fuck it, I thought. I wasn't about to ruin my Saturday because of some shitass musician who hated me, and whose name I knew. It was the longhair, Rodrigo. It could also be that faggot Nico. They could all go fuck themselves.

I sat in the living room, reading the paper, and it wasn't long before Jânia appeared, bringing me a cup of coffee. She tried to say something, but I pretended not to notice. I hid behind the newspaper, looking for articles about Israel. Now, for the first time, the United States was talking about the existence of a 'Palestinian state side by side with Israel'. There was a text backed by the UN calling for 'the immediate end to acts of violence, including acts of terror, provocation, incitement, and destruction'. That's a laugh, I thought. As if it were possible.

Marie woke up at 10:30. 'I want,' she said as we had sex that morning, 'I want to have your child.' I don't know if she'd say that if she knew I'd paid Jânia to spy on her.

After we bathed, I pretended that I felt like having a croissant for breakfast. 'I'll go buy some,' I said. As I left, I gestured to Jânia to go to her and tell everything. 'It has to be now. Tell her you threw out the newspapers. Unintentionally.' I didn't want to be there at the critical moment, fearing that my nervousness would give me away.

I went to the bakery and, upon my return, entered the apartment by the service door. 'I didn't tell her anything yet,' Jânia said. 'I was waiting for you to get back.'

'Tell her right now,' I ordered.

I went down to Rachel's apartment, and the maid opened the door. I handed her the bag of croissants that I'd bought. 'Make some tea and take these to Dona Rachel.'

'The pantry is empty,' the maid said. 'Dona Rachel never buys anything.' I got angry. Who asked her? I gave her some money. 'Go to the supermarket and fix something for her to eat. Can you come to work tomorrow?' I asked.

'Tomorrow's Sunday.'

'I'll pay double if you come every Sunday till she's out of the cast.'

When I returned home, I could hear my wife and Jânia arguing in the kitchen. Marie was furious.

'She threw out all my newspapers,' she told me as I came into the living room.

Jânia looked at me, smiling her usual smile, which seemed phlegmatic but in reality was pure threat. It was difficult to convince Marie not to fire her.

'Where am I going to find those articles about Israel? Those essays?'

I promised her that Adriana would help.

Marie went through the day with a scowl on her face. She thought everything was terrible. The restaurant 'full of nouveau riche', the traffic 'full of Sunday drivers', the DVD we rented; 'Woody Allen is a boring old man,' she commented sourly. But later, after smoking her joint, she recovered her good humor and completely forgot the episode with the newspapers.

That evening, Marie had the night off. We watched the Finn conduct the orchestra and later took him to dinner. There was a busybody at the table, whom Marie nicknamed Mrs. Boresly. A bore who only wanted to talk about music and who was certainly no musician, as she seemed not to know that among musicians, music is discussed as little as possible. We never talk about such things. It's a kind of faux pas to talk about music. We're like philosophers, we don't philosophize among ourselves. But, anyway, Mrs. Boresly amused us with her musical knowledge, so vast it would fit into a shopping bag. I assume the Finn ended up spending the night with her, despite the idiotic questions the woman had asked him. Was there a musical tradition in Finland? 'We have more opera singers than farm workers,' replied the maestro, who was also a gourmet. It was impressive: of every ten maestros I invited to conduct my orchestra, nine were gourmets. I had thought about becoming a gourmet myself.

The high point of the dinner was when Marie whispered in my ear if I had thought about what she'd said. 'Yes,' I replied, not knowing just what she was getting at. 'Are you game?' she said. I was game. I was game for everything. Only when she started talking about a surname and explaining why her parents were so insistent that I give up mine, did I understand that the subject was our child. Our child would carry her last name. Marie was an only child, and her parents wanted the family name to survive.

'You agree?'

From the look of things, everyone in that family would be Jewish. Except me.

7

NOT A SINGLE TREE, only asphalt. It wasn't yet ten in the morning, and the clock in Pacaembu stadium was showing eighty degrees. Summer in São Paulo is truly a terrible thing. No sooner does the sun come up than the city once again begins to rot before our very eyes. Everything is fermenting, effervescing, fetid in the heat, and not even at night, when a warm breeze blows or a rainstorm pours down, is it possible to avoid the malodorous smells of the metropolis. Only a great city like São Paulo can stink and rot in such a scandalous way. The outdoor markets and the tons of garbage we toss into the streets take on the task of achieving the full potential of the pestilent emanations. City workers hose down the locations after the markets are gone, and garbage pickup isn't all that slow, because we, the rich people, are demanding. But all of that, I mean, the cleaning up, the garbage collecting, and the rich, does absolutely no good when it comes to lessening the stench. The smell of fish and disinfectant is embedded in the asphalt. Without a little camphor in my nostrils I couldn't stand walking around those places, or anywhere else in São Paulo.

I parked the car and got out, carrying my football shoes over my shoulder. Pedro Ricardo, the coach, was in the dressing room with the musicians. It was a drag of a meeting. Why is that people in sports abuse clichés so much? It irritated me to see my musicians around him, listening to that string of drivel with the same attention they had given me days earlier as I explained Marcolini's theory of musical creation. 'Listen to this,' I'd said, with a book open in front of me, 'life is grand opera. The tenor and the baritone fight over the soprano, when it's not the soprano and the contralto fighting over the tenor. And God is the poet. He wrote the libretto, which Satan stole and set to music in Hell. And Earth is the theater. And we are the entire company, with all the roles, leading and supporting, chorus and dancers. And all of that is from Machado de Assis,' I said, showing them the book. 'Do some reading. A musician can't read only scores. You have to read Machado de Assis, Goethe. Read every day. Proust, William Carlos Williams, Isaac Bashevis Singer, read everything.' They had looked at me attentively, with curiosity, they had even asked questions about Machado. That brief conversation about literature had been a moment of peace between maestro and orchestra, a rare and spontaneous moment. They had played so well that day, I was so enthused, I liked seeing how they appreciated Machado de Assis's ideas on music, I was proud of my musicians, and for a minute, as rarely happened, I loved them as my children and thought, with a degree of vanity, that in the end my musicians were not gross, uncultured people but potential readers of Machado de Assis. That lasted two minutes – the harmony between us, I mean – and immediately I went back to seeing them as the idiots they were, and now the damned fools were there, finding Pedro Ricardo sensational with his rabble-rousing talk about how what mattered was to compete. And our coach didn't even look like a coach; he'd been a player in the past and now displayed a belly as prominent as mine. Maybe mine was a bit larger, but then I'd never been an athlete.

It was our first game, and our opponent was the Philharmonic. The last time I'd seen them was at the centenary celebrations of the death of Verdi. It had been depressing. I spent the entire concert looking at the shoes of the musicians onstage, thinking that they, the shoes, were the perfect portrait of classical music in Brazil: shabby, old, unpolished.

I had pitied the Philharmonic musicians so much that when Pedro Ricardo telephoned the previous week to set the date of the match I seriously considered whether it would be fair to compete with them. Whether it would be humiliating for them, and embarrassing for us. After all, my orchestra was a real orchestra. There were no gleaming shoes like those of Muti among my musicians, but they were shoes, our shoes. Leather shoes, with wooden heels. The girls wore clogs and open-toed sandals in the summer, low boots in the winter. They followed fashion, the women musicians. It wouldn't be fair of me to have the best orchestra and win the game on top of that. It would be uncomfortable to beat those poor losers and their perforated shoes. Would they play barefoot? 'I got Pacaembu,' Pedro Ricardo had told me, on that occasion. 'They're remodeling it, but for amateurs there's no problem.' I ended up accepting, and now here we were, in the dressing room.

I was going to Europe the next day. I had fought with Marie. 'Don't you know how to fold shirts?' I asked, when she tried to pack my suitcase. 'No,' she answered. 'I also don't know how to make beans, clean, wash clothes, or organize your press reviews. Maybe that bothers you a lot.' I didn't give a damn about beans. Or, for that matter, about poorly folded clothes, it was even fun to cram them into the suitcase. But that day everything was a pretext to quarrel with Marie. It gave me immense pleasure to shake her out of her seriousness. 'You're not modern,' I said. 'That stuff about not knowing how to fry an egg is so twentieth century. The modern woman is president of a multinational, goes to the supermarket, takes the kid to school, runs five miles a day, and prepares an unforgettable arugula and pine nut risotto.'

'Yes, I am from the last century, from the time when men didn't enslave their wives, from the time when they wanted to marry independent women, from the time when men weren't bothered by our lack of domestic skills –'

'You come from a generation of faggots,' I interrupted. 'Once you all started burning your bras, you've been taking nothing but abuse from men. Which of your boyfriends, other than me, ever opened the car door for you?'

Marie sighed in irritation. 'I don't give a damn.'

'Go on,' I insisted, 'give me a name, just one name. I want to know. All of them wore red pants and earrings, clogs, and had their feminine side. Never since the Middle Ages were women as mistreated as in the sixties. You've got a hard row to hoe.'

'What are you talking about?'

'Packing bags,' I replied.

'I'm not your secretary. Call Adriana if you want your clothes folded professionally,' said Marie, leaving the bedroom.

I phoned Adriana. I didn't give the slightest consideration mind to the foul mood that descended on our house upon the arrival of my secretary, her belly showing because of her piercing. 'It got infected,' she said. 'You think it looks bad?' It was pretty, but I didn't say so. There are people who would pay to lick that fake diamond. 'That girl's problem is that she's spoiled,' Adriana commented as we went to the bedroom to organize my bags. 'Just look at that mess. Everything thrown together. You're an artist, maestro.

You need someone to take care of you. Look at those socks. Those undershorts. You can't travel like that. Let me handle everything.'

Adriana went on with that litany, but I confess I wasn't listening anymore. I just wanted to get at Marie.

When I left the house, Marie was talking on the phone with her mother. She was speaking their language, but not exclusively; my wife wasn't fluent in Hebrew. Doubtless the two of them were complaining about me. The problem is that Marie would forget which words she taught me in bed. She also forgot that I had a good memory. Schnorrer. A bore, a whiner. That left me with a bad taste in my mouth.

In truth, I was depressed because Marie wasn't accompanying me on my European tour. I would serve as guest conductor in Florence, Madrid, and Amsterdam. In the time when we were lovers, we would talk a lot about 'always being together'. Teresa seldom accompanied me, I'd spent my life traveling by myself, packing my own bags, always alone, in hotels. I'd grown tired of that life, I wanted my wife with me, available, a companion. Marie had promised that she'd never leave me, she'd attend my rehearsals. I should have been suspicious of so many promises. Now 'the situation has changed', she'd said, when she told me she wasn't going with me anymore. She had been hired by my orchestra, she had eight concerts in that period, and she considered it 'unprofessional to drop everything to travel with you'. Of course, since I was artistic director it would have been no problem to find a substitute violinist, but she, with Cláudio's backing, insisted 'it wasn't professional'. I myself didn't consider it 'professional', in fact, but even less professional was Marie's continuing in the orchestra after we had decided to live together. Still, what annoyed me was the fact of her repeating with such intensity the word *professional.*

'Then resign,' I suggested, exasperated. She and Cláudio laughed, as if I were joking. I myself laughed and pretended I wasn't serious. But I was disappointed, and lost the desire to conduct in Europe. I don't know what bothered me more, the idea of traveling by myself, all that hassle of planes and airports, or realizing just how independent Marie was.

'I have eight concerts,' she'd said, as if eight concerts were much more important than the two of us and our life.

I became very unstable in the days preceding the trip. I fired Rodrigo from the orchestra because he came in twenty minutes late. I was quite rigorous in regard to discipline, but I don't think I would have let the young man go if I didn't suspect him of being the person who had called my house to speak to Marie, as Jânia had told me. It was a good feeling when Adriana came to me and said it had blown him away. At least, at first it was good. Later I felt guilty and couldn't sleep at night. Rodrigo had an eleven-month-old daughter and his wife was out of work. I called him in the next day and rehired him.

Now, before the game, he avoided speaking to me. I'm not sure, but I think I heard him comment to a flute player something about and-on-top-of-everything-else-he-wants-to-be-goalie.

We went out onto the field, in silence. The other team seemed to be having a good time, running on boisterously behind their concertmaster. I knew their concertmaster, a lousy concertmaster, by the way. They used a bottle of mineral water to wet down the youth. They laughed a lot. We, the opposing team, watched the scene, laughing also. I mean, I didn't laugh, not finding the least thing funny about any of it; I wanted to play. The Philharmonic musicians were in uniforms, which was surprising. Much better uniforms than ours. In fact, with the exception of my goalie's gloves, my special shoes, and my satiny black jersey that I had ordered from Cláudio by phone on his way back from Toronto, our opponents' uniforms were vastly superior to ours. The guys had a shitty orchestra, but no one could tell that by looking at their blue shorts with green stripes.

Ten minutes into the game they scored their first goal. I wasn't focused. Why hadn't Marie wanted to travel with me? Men who demand that their wives let go of everything are ridiculous. I've always hated that kind of man. I always blamed myself because Teresa had done so. It was still painful to remember a day from many years earlier, in a rugged Boston winter, when I came home and found her, happy and resigned, washing our clothes, kneeling beside the bathtub. I had won a fellowship to do my Ph.D. in musicology and Teresa had given up her career as soloist to go with me. We lived without money and our apartment was so small we didn't even have a washtub. The wet clothes were hung over the heaters, and Teresa did all that on her own, while pregnant. She never complained. Just the opposite – her attitude was positive, encouraging. 'Concentrate on your music,' she would say. 'Leave the rest to me.' And I did. All the small stuff. That day I didn't have classes and had spent the afternoon at the movies with a female friend. I felt really miserable when I saw Teresa's altruism, but not to the point of canceling my meeting the next day with the same friend. Even now, when I remember, I feel like calling her and apologizing. I didn't want Marie to give up her obligations in Brazil. But neither did I want her not to accompany me. Or for her to repeat, so enthusiastically, phrases like 'my violin', 'my career', 'my future', 'my plans'.

They scored the second goal on me because of these

thoughts. I saw the play forming in front of me, a fucker on the Philharmonic team caught the ball on his chest, got set, and kicked. The save would have been easy if I were paying attention. But I couldn't manage to grab the ball. I stood there, I'm not sure but I think I even might have had my arms crossed at the moment of the goal.

At halftime, when I entered the dressing room, the musicians were furious with me. A horrible atmosphere. I felt so uneasy, so shaken up, that I wouldn't be able to tend goal in the second half. I took a cold shower and went to talk to Pedro Ricardo. 'I don't think that's a good idea,' he said when I told him. 'The purpose of this game is to bring the team together.'

'One more reason for me to give up the goalie position,' I explained. Pedro Ricardo didn't like it. Maybe the musicians wouldn't like it either. I myself didn't like it, I was so angry that I played the rest of the game at left half and gave my musicians some good kicks. I landed some of them on Rodrigo.

Afterward, in the dressing room, to excuse myself I said that football was a game of impact, of collision, of physical contact.

Pedro Ricardo was very unhappy, I knew. The musicians barely looked at me. I thought about inviting everyone to lunch, but Marie hated the idea. 'You go,' she said, 'I'm just not up to it.' To tell the truth, neither was I. I went home with a feeling of total disintegration. I recalled that talk of Pedro Ricardo's about uniting the team. Three to nothing in favor of the Philharmonic. Our first game had ended very badly.

8

'I SEE AND APPROVE the better things but follow the worse.' I don't quite know where I read that sentence of Ovid's, and in fact I'm not even sure it was Ovid, but in any case it was no accident that he came galloping into my mind. It was exactly what was happening with me at that moment. Approving the better and destroying everything. Screwing up time after time. Following the worse. Having great clarity about the situation, excellent ideas, and then fouling it all up in practice. I knew I was crossing the line, that my attitudes were, to say the least, worthy of censure, but nevertheless I was simply unable to stop.

'You ought to hit me,' I told Marie on Saturday night, when we returned from dinner at her parents' house, where I had caused a horrendous scene. She didn't even answer me, but locked herself in the bedroom to smoke marijuana while I stayed in the living room, pacing, repentant.

I had acted improperly with Henri and Monique. When we arrived, some friends of the family were there, all of them rich, most of them Jewish, and the topic was the 'demonstrations', the term used by Arabs to denote the activity of throwing rocks at Israeli soldiers. In some Palestinian cities, they said, there was now a profession called 'demonstration coordinator'. Boys who met after school in bands of fifty or sixty and went out stoning Israelis. 'That's a trend,' stated one of the Jews, a banker, 'the truth is that more and more, the radical Islamic movements have the support of the Palestinian population.' This was the opinion of a terrorism specialist at the University of Jerusalem, the banker explained. And his own, obviously. What impressed me was when another friend, a businessman, told us that in less than a year almost forty militants from radical movements spontaneously volunteered to be suicide bombers. 'An extremely high number,' he said. I started thinking about the type of guy who decides to become a suicide bomber. I made some comment or other, they looked at me curiously. I said I was interested in suicide bombers. 'In the phenomenon,' I added. Then, to put an end to the topic for good, I asked if the mortality figures for Arab children were true. What did they think? I don't know why I butted into that conversation. Actually, I had always been irritated by Jewish autism at dinners at Marie's parents' house. How they loved to talk about the Jews. Wasn't there some other topic? It vexed me. And I couldn't avoid it.

Then came the worst part. I told Marie my opinion of the guests. 'Are you aware of the pathological nature of the group? The rich are like psychotics, they establish a nucleus and attribute roles to each member. Each group has a maestro. And a jester. A courtesan. A banker. A president of a holding company. You're the talented young woman,' I had said.

Marie tried to escape my claws by attempting to talk to the guests, but I kept dragging her away from the Jews to tell her that the American sickness had finally made it to Brazil. 'Interesting rich people. Rich people who read, listen to music, and don't spout nonsense. They don't make the rich like they used to, and that's the truth. In the old days the rich would go out and hunt lions, cut down forests, and pollute the oceans. Nowadays they do worse things, but they're full of guilt, they belong to NGOs, and love to use words like *excluded*, *multiculturalism*, *minorities*, and everything else.'

I also told Marie that all those 'friends of your father' had in common, besides being Jewish and rich, was the fact of owning private jets, complete with flight attendant. And that however much they tried to appear deprived, there was a pile of dollars hanging on every sentence they uttered.

Marie was silent on our way home; actually, she had been mute from the moment when, at the table, I couldn't stop from asking if everyone there had a private plane. One of them, the holding company president, had the gall to reply, 'Our firm does.' That was prior to my raising the topic of Arab children. The rich are sophists and hypocrites. I also said that to Marie. 'They like to pose as leftists, to say they're concerned about maldistribution of income, but they don't do a goddamn thing. They just make more money.'

In the car, I couldn't stop talking. 'The truth is, I hate the rich. Collectors of anything. Good wines, exotic voyages. That kind of thing. Those people. Those women, those topics. I hate all that,' I told Marie. 'And don't think I'm like them, that I love the poor. I have a deep-seated disdain for the poor. The rabble. The scum. Dirty, ignorant, self-seeking, immoral. Filthy, like worms. Always getting pregnant. And getting fat. And robbing and killing. And getting run over. I think I hate the poor even more. That's not true. I hate the rich more. At least the rabble move me.'

Earlier, I had made an enormous scene and then gone off to wander around the rooms, avoiding the guests in a flagrantly spiteful manner. I had the impression that the pantryman's function was to be my page. 'Is there something you'd like, sir?' he asked, more than twice. 'Your house,' I told Monique when she came looking for me, 'your house is very noisy. There are lots of dogs barking, and that puts me on edge. Noise is a form of poison.' She was embarrassed by my comments and even stopped saying to her women friends that foolishness about 'my son-in-law' and 'talented conductor'. 'I can't eat with all this noise,' I said, though there wasn't any barking at all. The only thing to be heard in that house, besides the background music, was Marie's laughter. Marijuana always made her laugh a lot. 'When you arrive in Israel,' she said, 'the first thing they ask is whether you know what's the second language of the land. Everybody thinks it's Russian. The number of Russians is growing all the time. "No," they say, "it's Hebrew." That's their favorite joke.' 'Now tell that other one, Sandorsky's,' I said from the living room. They quieted down, waiting. Marie appeared embarrassed. They stopped laughing.

In the car, the effect of the marijuana had run its course.

'Why don't "those people" fly in commercial airlines?' I asked Marie.

'Because we're rich,' she replied, irritated. 'And because we're not like you, we don't read Cioran.'

'I've never read Cioran.'

'No? I thought you liked that business about I-don't-kill-myself-because-suicide-is-always-within-my-grasp, killing-myself-is-the-easiest-thing-in-the-world. After reading Cioran, you're going to start telling everybody that he's the only one who's any good.'

That's all she said. Nothing more. I understood everything. I shut up for the rest of the drive and opened my mouth only to say that Marie was absolutely right, to apologize, to say that, deep down, I must be resentful, have an inferiority complex to utter all that nonsense that way, 'It's all one huge piece of stupidity,' I concluded.

When I look back on that period of my life I also remember the feeling of hatred that enveloped me, how anything would fill me with rage and impotence. Nor did Marie escape from that fury. If we weren't wrapped around each other, if she wasn't adoring me, my feelings in relation to her were rather ambiguous. On my part there was constant disapproval, as if Marie were about to be co-opted by enemies. If the topic was the Jewish reality, like at that dinner, or if, in a more prosaic situation, some Sunday afternoon while organizing her drawers, Marie suddenly came upon old photos, photos of her with her girlfriends, playing tennis or camping, laughing, happy, vigorous, I was overcome by a sense of unease, an inexplicable, confused feeling, a mixture of suffering and rage. What was it about those happy expressions and sundaes at the shopping center that made me so melancholy? It was some time before I understood what was going on with me. Me. I myself wasn't there. That's what I saw, my absence. I couldn't bear not being there. Not belonging. Not being part of it. Remaining behind. Coming later. Not being present. That hit me, like a blow. By then it did no good to try to explain anything to Marie, after I had made such a scene at the dinner.

It was almost midnight when I decided to organize the scores that I'd take on the trip. I called Adriana. 'They're here with me, I was going to bring them to you, tomorrow at the airport.' I asked her to leave them with her doorman, I didn't want her to meet me at the airport. When I got to her building, there was nothing for me in the lobby. I was forced to go up. It wasn't a good idea, I knew that. There was practically no furniture in the living room, just a large table piled high with papers, and that's why we went directly to her bedroom. First we stopped by the kitchen and got Diet Cokes with ice and lime.

'Look at this,' she said, rewinding the tape to show a scene in a film. Christ dancing to the sound of Beethoven's Ninth. 'Isn't that fantastic? I love that director, I've seen everything he's ever done.' I ended up watching the film with her, lying on the bed. We were side by side, Adriana in shorts, sometimes I stole a glance at her legs, gauging the marks my sharp teeth would make on that flesh. I didn't move a muscle. It was she who took the initiative, sticking her tongue into my mouth. Her lips were cold from the drink. The doorbell rang. Adriana leapt from the bed, and I heard her say in surprise, 'Wasn't it supposed to be tomorrow?' No, no it wasn't. It was today, explained a male voice. Her boyfriend was really irritated when he saw me coming out of the bedroom. 'They're all here, maestro,' Adriana said, handing me a package. Suddenly, I was the maestro. 'Maestro,' she continued. 'If maestro wishes.' 'All the scores, Ravel, Barber, Saint-Saëns, I've checked them all.' Almost two in the morning. I got the scores and left.

The way back was horrible, a sensation of guilt took hold. There's nothing to be done, I began repeating, and suddenly, in the midst of all that confusion, I managed to articulate mentally a convincing speech to persuade Marie to forgive me. For one moment everything seemed simple, I felt an enormous sense of peace, everything would work out well once I had apologized to Marie. I even thought that perhaps it might be worthwhile to call her parents' home and also apologize to them. That stuff about the airplane, I could say, on second thought, it's very good to have a plane. Better not to go into details. Simply apologize.

But when I got home I no longer remembered the speech. I felt totally exhausted. The idea of the flight the next day, the tour, the smell of the airplane, the smell of the hotels, the dinners following the concert, and, especially, the imminent separation from Marie, all of that would be the end of me.

9

TURIN, GENEVA, TRIESTE, AND NAPLES, that was my itinerary. The advantage of a European tour over an American one is that with the former you arrive at the airports and there's no one from the orchestra waiting to take you to the hotel. It's something not to have to engage in conversation with a volunteer after a twelve-hour flight. They're the housewives of the orchestra, the volunteers. Responsible for the small stuff.

Knowing that in the Old World you're free of them, at least on your way to the hotel, and that it's possible to make the airport-to-hotel stretch in the most civilized manner conceivable – in other words, getting a taxi by yourself, with your bags and your awful thoughts and your fear of conducting badly – was in itself a relief. I felt very insecure in relation to new orchestras. If the hotel wasn't a good one, if the musicians didn't receive me with enthusiasm, I quickly began to doubt my competence. I've never managed to overcome that. I was always afraid of opening the newspaper and reading an article of the conductor-charlatan-exposed type.

At the first rehearsal, I remembered what it's like to conduct in Italy. The snare drums were for shit. The violins, crummy as always. The rest played well, they would come and go, never caring about what was being played beside them. But always very nice. A lovable, shitty group. The famous so-bad-it's-good style.

Arrival at the hotel had been memorable. There was no traffic, but that was no help because the traffic lights in Turin don't let you move. One after the other. The taxi driver explained to me that the brother of the previous mayor owned a factory that made traffic lights. 'That's Turin for you,' he said.

I didn't want to travel, I had spent the night thinking about some way of canceling the trip, and I had even called my agent in England to ask what could be done. Agents simply can't take it when you call to speak of personal problems. 'Well,' Freddy told me sarcastically, 'unless you've got some tropical disease, the best thing's for you to show up and conduct.'

Shortly before I left, I was so irritated that I kicked the wall to see if it would calm me down. Adriana had left a series of scores for my tour at the theater, and the laptop fell from my hand as I was storing it in my suitcase. And Marie remained ensconced in the bedroom, after making me spend the night in the living room.

'Sixty-five percent of American Jews who go to college marry Gentiles. Sixty-five percent lost forever to the Jewish people. This is why young people are learning Hebrew in Agor. To get away from Jewish indifference, from the coming extinction of Jews in the United States.' During my sleepless night I had reread that and other passages underlined in red ink in the book Marie had left on my piano.

Few things tore me up more than realizing, in such situations, that important parts of Marie were escaping me. My musical Marie, available and lovable, was underlining, in books by her favorite authors, sentences about mixed marriages bringing about a second Holocaust, sentences that were probably the manifestation of her own opinions.

It was that Marie, secretive, intractable, who made me unstable. Why had she underlined that sentence? Was that her opinion too? We never spoke about 'mixed marriages' or 'Jewish indifference'. Or about the fact that I wasn't Jewish. 'I never understood what it meant to be Jewish until I went to Israel,' she'd once said. 'I didn't grow up in a Jewish neighborhood. I never had religious instruction. I grew up in São Paulo, I studied in schools where being Jewish meant more than anything else being rich. The trip had for me the same significance that the synagogue had for my grandparents. I still remember the day I visited the Wailing Wall. It was a Friday and I was with a girlfriend who was studying sociology at the University of Jerusalem and who, like me, is Brazilian and Jewish. I remember that Sofia told me she envied me the emotions I would experience by living in Israel. "It's unavoidable," she said, "suddenly you discover what it means to belong to something. Even if you've never cared in the least about it, even if you don't want to understand, even if you think none of it means anything to you. The thing simply falls on your head. Here, you're going to understand everything, even what you never thought about wanting to comprehend." When I heard that, I felt a kind of inferiority at my inability to be moved by Israel in the same way my friend was moved, because I was unable to recognize myself the way she had recognized herself in that place. All I'd felt till that moment had been fear. I had visited the central marketplace with my father's cousin, who belonged to the secret service and gave me an armed escort. It was horrible. But, in short, I truly believed that my life in Israel would be the life of a foreigner, and it was then that I began hearing very melodious music, approaching closer and closer, and soon I ran into a group of Hassidim welcoming the Shabbat, chanting, in their black clothing. It was enough. I was so moved that I started crying. It was as if the melody said to me: "you belong here".'

When Marie told me of her life in Israel, I realized I could never share that with her, that my life had been a history of normality, normal parents, normal middle-class Brazilian family, without any record of conquests or failures, without anything about which to feel pride, normal people with normal Sundays, filled with boredom in an insipid city, surrounded by uninteresting people, people I never saw again, without anything singular, without any emotion. Practically a nothing. It meant absolutely nothing to me to belong to a Catholic family. The rituals, the prayers, nothing. My parents didn't care a bit. Much less me. All that remained of my religious life was the memory of first communion, confession, the priest telling me that I was free of my sins and my having thought that it was all too simple. It was only a matter of asking forgiveness. Sin and ask for forgiveness. And the payoff was always absolution, because in the final analysis God was a fool.

In sum, all this is to say how excluded from Marie's life I felt. Even the fact of our never having spoken of my non-belonging to the Jewish world meant something. What is left unsaid is what's real. It's that which chafes. Which corrodes. I was weary of having only her exterior, and I thought about telling her so, that day before leaving for the airport. Marie remained locked in the bedroom, in silence, wounded because I'd been rude to her parents, to her family. I'm tired of being on the outside, staying here outside, I thought of saying. Come out of there right now, I felt like shouting. But I kept up my policy of reconciliation. 'If you were offended yesterday at your parents' by that business about Arab children, I want you to know I'm one hundred percent against the Intifada,' I yelled from the living room, while rummaging through the bookcases in search of the scores. How could Adriana have forgotten them? Unbelievable, the incompetence of people. 'I think the Intifada is stupid,' I went on. 'I even think that those Arabs don't give a damn about plans for the creation of a Palestinian state. What they want is to kill Jews.' Forgetting the third *Bachiana*, of all things; Adriana was an idiot. 'Marie, could you see if the *Bachiana #3* is in there somewhere?' I said, pressed against the door of our bedroom. 'Maybe it's in my bookcase.' I insisted she look for it. Nothing.

It took a long time for me to lose my patience, but suddenly my blood boiled, I threatened to throw Marie's violin out the window, I shouted, kicked doors, made so much noise that the doorman rang the bell and asked if there was a problem.

'The doorman thinks I'm going to kill you, Marie,' I said, after apologizing for the incident and sending him away.

Marie soon opened the door. She was barefoot and in pajamas.

'Come here,' she said.

I went over to Marie. Are you going to forgive me? I thought of asking her, but she hugged me. We stood there silently for some time, then we got into bed, hurriedly, panting, longing, and had what Marie called 'our ultra-frenetic goodbye'. In general, after that orgasmic peace, I would fall into a kind of stupor, feel exhausted, but drained of the poisons in me and quite calm.

Marie didn't mention the scene I had caused the night

before, and that pacified me. Neither criticism nor forgiveness was going to solve anything. I felt incapable of not hurting her again. I knew that in a short time I would once again be poisoned, full of fury; my behavior was like a wheel moving back and forth, building and demolishing, constructing and conquering, only to later destroy it all.

But suddenly, on the way to the airport, I finally understood that Marie was part of that perverse cycle. It didn't matter what might happen. It didn't matter how badly everything went. How disappointed she might be. How much I wounded myself. How much flesh was left behind on the barbed wire. We had a pact. An anti-explosion, anti-black-bile, anti-fury, anti-separation pact. Nothing would affect us. She belonged to me and I to her. Forever.

Teresa, at the wheel, with her traditional sourness, couldn't alter my mood. Our daughter had decided to go to Europe with me. There she was, in the car, with her adolescent awkwardness, wanting to show us the camera she'd bought for the occasion. But Teresa, wielding her cudgel of unpleasant words, was disinclined to let her talk. I'm not sure, but I assume that all the talk about guest conductors for my orchestra was in order to insinuate that my international career was due solely to what she called the 'exchange system'. We maestros traded favors, which is why we were always traveling. Teresa had what she considered an 'indirect' way of saying things. She asked if I planned to study the score on the plane. It was as if she were saying *See how easy it is to be a conductor*. A scam. None of you even prepare anymore. You go there and conduct, nothing else. Any which way. Without the least consideration for the music and the public. I didn't let Teresa continue with her blah-blah-blah, the significance of which was the insignificance of my profession. I'd already seen that film. I asked Eduarda to show me how to use the camera.

We got to the airport late and almost missed the flight. Eduarda still wanted to buy some magazines. I stood at the gate, complaining to Teresa and hurrying my daughter.

It was a long trip.

10

WHEN I LIVED IN GERMANY, studying conducting, I was impressed by the number of marvelous children in the city and by the infinitely larger number of dreadful adults. After a time, I almost couldn't refrain from attentively watching those extraordinarily beautiful children, only to immediately have the perverse pleasure of substantiating, through study of their obese mothers, red as tomatoes, that they would become 'that there', that horror, or something even worse. I never liked children, to tell the truth. I was always astonished by the quickness with which they learn to lie, cheat, become hypocritical and selfish, and the rapidity with which they are transformed into idiotic adults, like all of us. Besides which, children are born and marriages end. They fulfill the woman, never the man. It was no different with Teresa and me. Eduarda was born and voraciously took over her mother. I loved my daughter, of course, but in a confused way. Fatherhood always inspired contradictory feelings in me. The idea of being a father was pleasant, but to me the physical presence of a baby in our house was unbearable. Her fragility was frightening. I was afraid of Eduarda. Afraid of killing her, especially. Of crushing her, of dropping her and stepping on her head. During her early years, I was incapable of holding her in my arms, or even getting very close to her. Nevertheless, I developed an obsessive concern about her health. I wouldn't allow anyone but Teresa to pick her up, fearing that their germs would lodge in my daughter. Furniture, objects, doorknobs – everything had to be disinfected after visitors left, indignant at having to wear surgical masks in my house.

Later, when Eduarda had grown a little, my obsessions ceased. I calmed down. I got closer to my daughter, became more affectionate, but not excessively so. It was good to have that healthy girl calling me Daddy and then leaving me in peace. I was what might be called a 'professional father', an absent presence. I wasn't there, but it was as if I were.

So when Eduarda phoned to say she wanted to accompany me on my European tour, I was desperate. 'Why travel with me?' I asked, distressed. 'It's my birthday,' she answered. 'Throw a party,' I suggested. But my daughter wanted to see Europe. I tried to convince her that almost all of Europe was just old and musty. 'Traveling is always a drag,' I said, 'the airports are infernal, full of terrorists and bomb-sniffing dogs, I don't think it's a good idea for you to go with me.' It was Teresa, with her theory that my 'pathological selfishness' was going to 'totally fuck me', who made me agree to take Eduarda. 'She's giving you one last chance. Take it or leave it.'

What could I do with my daughter? Where to put her? How to rid myself of her presence during rehearsals? Where would I find the patience to listen to her rambling stories? I pictured her with her nose in a Michelin guide, repeating phrases like 'Salzburg is the Rome of Germany' or 'Amsterdam is the Dutch Venice', forcing me to visit tourist spots full of Japanese. There are rules, I thought about saying. It's forbidden to get lost, forbidden to wake me up, to interrupt me, to ask for things, forbidden to talk too much, forbidden to want difficult things, forbidden to invite me to eat fast food, forbidden to be a shopping tourist – I made a huge list, but it wasn't necessary to say any of it. The truth is that I didn't really know Eduarda. I knew nothing about her.

Eduarda endured anything, was interested in anything, would reject anything, try anything, wanted everything, laughed at everything, and was game for everything. In truth, she was sensational. 'I prefer to be with my father,' she said, in a delightfully obstinate and childish way, when someone suggested an alternative program, during the rehearsals. And being with me meant literally being with me. Attending my rehearsals and concerts, eating at my favorite restaurants with the bores of all types who accompany me on such occasions, bores who don't talk, bores who talk too much, ignorant bores, learned bores, bores who collect all kinds of nonsense. In a word, musicians in general. I never thought I would like being with my daughter so much, listening to her radical opinions about anything, and her spirited guffaws.

By that time I no longer had any patience with certain European orchestras, with 'bovine musicians', as I came to call them. They were lifeless on the stage, playing without emotion. At the first rehearsal they would impress by their virtuosity. At the last one, by their ability to remain stuck in the same place, getting neither better nor worse, not feeling anything. Cattle stuck in the mud. They know how to play, but detest what they do. And that's not exclusively European musicians. In the United States the situation is even worse. Americans, even those in the Big Five, hate being orchestral musicians. It's the most execrated profession in the country, even more than that of prison guard. And it's very unpleasant to conduct those bureaucrats, especially when their talent is eroded by the lowest-common-denominator of the vulgar.

They can get away with anything, the musicians of Geneva. They can be absent, arrive late, they can even get Beethoven's Eighth wrong, precisely because they can never be fired. Some have been there for fifteen years. Fifteen years doing that, with all that Swiss emotion. It was common, at the end of rehearsals, for me to phone my agent in England and ask just why I had to conduct those orchestras. 'Because you're a conductor,' Freddy would answer, 'and because you're not in the category of an old master who can choose whom he tells to go to hell.' I didn't think like Freddy. The truth is that I knew why I was there; I was there because I was Brazilian. If you want to be a musician in Brazil you have to leave the country. Brazil doesn't respect anyone who opts to stay. To be respected as a conductor here you practically have to turn your back on Brazil. It's part of the business, as I learned early on.

But the fact is that Eduarda ended up being responsible for one of my best presentations in Europe. It was her birthday, and I wanted to dedicate the Geneva concert, in Victoria Hall, to her. The mud-bound herd of cattle planned on giving me only that insipid Swiss musical technique. We fought a battle, I and the musicians. 'You don't like me,' I said, 'and I don't like you. I promise I'll never come back. But you have to play my way.' In the rehearsals I was like a tormented animal, I was the musicians' worst nightmare, they hated me, I know, but only until the day of the concert. At the end of our first performance, as the applause from the audience echoed, they discreetly stamped their feet, still sitting in their chairs, demonstrating contentment and admiration.

I know Eduarda enjoyed the concert. I'll never forget our embrace, emotional and silent, and our stroll to the restaurant, where we had dinner to celebrate her fourteenth birthday. 'You know something, Dad,' she said, 'we could travel together more often.'

I had a week off and took Eduarda to see Rome, where I had lived for a few years in my youth. I was so anxious to show my daughter the city that the day after our arrival I already had blisters on my feet. 'Dad, you could write one of those every-corner-of-Rome guidebooks.' We walked the entire length of Via Giulia, from the bridge designed by Michelangelo, which connected the Farnese Palace and Villa Farnesina, to the Florentine church, seeing everything, without haste, Sangallo's house, Michelangelo's, Caravaggio's frescoes in Rizzi's castle, the Museum of Crime, the galleries – in short, it was very enjoyable. Teresa had never been a good traveling companion, what she liked was shopping, looking at store windows. And Marie wasn't curious like Eduarda. In the morning we would decide what we wanted to do, and then spend all day in the streets, 'searching out every cranny in Rome', as Eduarda had put it. 'We can do our own Michelin, Dad. Seriously. Rome in Twelve Years. Because at this rate, stopping to look at every insignificant detail, we'd have to live here.' By the fifth day of the trip she no longer was quite so lively. 'We spend all day in the street, Dad, without taking advantage of the hotel. Let's sleep till later. Have breakfast in our room. They have films to rent. I can't take seeing one more church, piazza, ruin or statue of Bernini. I don't know anymore who Sangallo was, which church is Santa Maria in Cosmedin, which one is Santa Maria in Campitelli, who did what, I've forgotten what's Romanesque, what's Gothic, the styles, my head's about to explode.'

Our days in Rome were the best part of the trip. I was calm, slept well, and was focused on my work. I almost didn't think about Marie. I felt almost no love for her. To tell the truth, it was as if Marie didn't even exist, and I hadn't the slightest need to speak with her. She would sometimes phone me late at night, getting me out of bed, probably high on marijuana, to say sickly-sweet things. 'Tell me you love me,' she'd say, 'tell me you want to go to bed with me, tell me that without me you're fucked.' At that moment, it didn't make the least bit of sense to repeat that nonsense. I wasn't fucked, I was focused and conducting very well. Conducting with so much enthusiasm that it had affected even the Swiss musicians. 'Our timbre changed, maestro, after you came,' they said. 'Brazilian Maestro Reveals the Beauty of Latin American Composition' was what it said in the newspapers. No one can speak of Brazilian music without emphasizing our exotic Latinity. We carry Brazil on our backs, we Brazilians. But, in any case, I wasn't even a little fucked. I was out of patience with Marie. Especially the day she said: 'I've got something to tell you; we're going to Chile with my father, next holiday. He invited us and is paying all the expenses. It'll be great, you need to rest, we'll take some of your scores, books, and we can go hiking every day. I've checked with Adriana, and you have no concerts that week. My cousin Fanny is going also. And her boyfriend, who's an artist in New York, according to my mother a very interesting young man. And what about you? What's new?' 'Go to Chile by yourself,' I replied. Marie slammed the phone down. But the next day there were messages on the answering machine in the bedroom, some really idiotic messages: 'Good morning, you ingrate, just a call to say I'm thinking of you', 'Just to say I love you', 'Just to say that you're not going to get away from me'. And they continued to get worse. 'I'm hurt. Why aren't you calling me anymore?' Great, I thought: the same-old, same-old begins. Here comes the little woman. Hurt. That irritated me no end. I can't explain why. Maybe because I imagined that we had barely begun our story and all that crap was already coalescing around us.

That was how I felt. And then, suddenly, things turned bad. It was in Trieste, just after my concert. We were at the hotel, Eduarda was sleeping in the bedroom next door, I wasn't sleepy. I can never sleep after a concert. The music stays in my head for a long time. It was past three in the morning, I was reading an article about a Palestinian suicide bomber blowing himself up. Since Marie, the main priority in my reading was the conflict in the Middle East. Four days after the accident, the article said, three suicide bombers had killed twenty-five Jews. And three days after that, another suicide bomber blew up three Jews at a bus stop almost at the same time that, in another part of the city, Jewish soldiers killed two Palestinians. And two days after that, two Palestinians killed two Jews in a train station and were immediately killed by Jews. It was because of the article that I decided to call Marie. She was always saying that she wanted to understand that hatred. The explanation was there. The ricochet effect. Everybody kills everybody. The reason no longer mattered. That's why I called Marie. To talk about the war. No one answered at home. And it was eleven p.m. in Brazil. And later, at eleven-ten, the telephone went on ringing, endlessly. Eleven-thirty, midnight, two, three, five in the morning. Nothing. The cell phone, the first time I tried it, went unanswered. After that, the calls went directly to the message box.

In less than half an hour I returned to that old state of unease and my old self, vulnerable and unprotected, went into action with impressive rapidity. What was going on? I wondered. It was as if, suddenly, my entire brain were eaten away. There was nothing propping me up, I could neither sit nor stand. Horrible images rushed through my mind. Marie murmuring, moaning, our words, spoken in bed, but it wasn't me she was speaking to, I wasn't there, there was someone else in my place. Everything we did together she was also doing with others, with someone from her world, a Jew, a musician from the orchestra, a stranger, an enemy. Someone her own age. I thought about Adriana. My secretary was also in a serious relationship. But that didn't stop her from showing me her pierced navel, or sticking her tongue in my mouth at the first opportunity. I remembered our last conversation, when I called Brazil to ask how things were going in the orchestra.

'I loved it when you kissed me,' she said.

'I didn't kiss you,' I replied.

'No? Then what was that in my bed?'

'You stuck your tongue in my mouth.'

'Really? What an invasive, unhygienic thing, sticking your tongue in someone else's mouth. I never thought I could do it. You ought to fire me, maestro.'

Women do that. They betray. And so do men. We fuck the people we love. That's the rule, and it applies to everyone, to me, to Adriana, why shouldn't it apply to Marie? I spent the night calling home. The TV showed nothing but images of war, 'American friendly fire,' said the reporter, explaining that the United States had hit its own tail with what they call a smart bomb.

I still had another concert in Naples. By seven I had already taken a shower, arranging everything by phone. I spoke to my agent in London; it wasn't hard to find a substitute conductor. There's no shortage of available conductors.

I went to the airport, taking my daughter, not knowing if I'd be able to leave. The flights to Brazil were all booked. I ended up going to Lisbon, sleeping in a horrendous hotel and catching a morning flight to Brazil. On the plane I was like a wild animal. I was a real handful for Eduarda, and I think she finally learned not to ask to travel with me again.

I arrived in São Paulo at five in the afternoon. There was a heavy rain, the sky was dark, and my feeling was that things were going to get a lot worse.

II

I SPLASHED WATER ON my face and looked at myself in the mirror. I bared my teeth. 'You look awful,' Teresa had said minutes before, when she met us in the waiting area at the airport. And she'd added: 'Next time you change your plans, don't be so selfish.'

I wasn't happy about the scene with Teresa. We had already argued when I phoned from Portugal to tell her that Eduarda and I would be returning early. 'You just ruined my weekend,' she said. She was planning to 'travel with friends' and would have to cancel because of our sudden return.

These days that was how Teresa acted. She used words like 'a philosophy study group' and 'Northern Coastline' in an especially affected way, as weapons to offend me, words that went perfectly with the high heels and extravagant rings she now wore. She was slimmer, I noticed. And more muscular. And taller too. My impression was that Teresa had grown a few inches since our separation. And that she had nothing more to say to me except that I looked awful.

It was sad to say goodbye to my daughter. Our trip hadn't ended well; I'd been impatient with her, particularly on the flight. 'Think, Eduarda,' I'd said, 'before asking me idiotic questions.' 'Don't try my patience.' And when she had wanted to confirm that it really was a ten-hour flight, right after the announcement from the cockpit, I couldn't restrain my irritation. 'Isn't that what they just said? If they say it's ten hours, it's because it's ten hours. Or do you think they're trying to fool us?' In these situations, Eduarda didn't react, showed no signs of hurt. In that too we were alike. We had, both of us, what I called a 'wall'. A wall there inside, behind the face, that let nothing escape. Nothing leaked out, no information, no feeling. At her age I was exactly the same, I was quite capable of listening to sheer nonsense and ignoring it. I knew how to remain immobile and also invisible. I had rescued myself from that immobility by becoming a conductor. Impermeable. By developing an odd way of loving others. But Eduarda still didn't know how to defend herself. She assimilated my scoldings in a delicate way, and nothing in her sweet features changed. When we said goodbye, I thought about saying something about 'the next time', but I felt it better to keep quiet. I didn't want to commit myself.

Teresa was right. I really did look horrible. The smell of bathroom at the airport made me feel even worse. With globalization, everything bad became the same the world over, the outskirts, the airports, and hotel lobbies and also the smells. A globalized smell of disinfectant, air conditioning and lavender. My camphor had run out, as I'd used the last of it on the return flight to Brazil.

I stopped at a pharmacy and bought more camphor, then went to the departure terminal. It was early for my plans, I thought, although I wasn't yet sure what my plans were. I wandered about a bit, aimlessly, irritated at the movement around me. The flying riffraff, an enormous mass equipped with cell phones, talking about warranty conditions, supply, accessories, term of coverage. 'We want a separate written contract, you hear?' 'The problems are the result of the timetable.' And the names they say, like Odair, Ednéia, Amílton, 'It's your call, Ivaldo.' I started imagining what Ivaldo's call would be, at the other end of the connection. The airport was a corral. The cattle, managers, businessmen, rabble, marketing directors. 'We'll take a meeting, Omar, with the Geresa people at the DIP.' 'He's the CEO at Pix.' Noisy animals. I tried to get away from the crowd by going into a bookstore. But there was an even bigger agglomeration buying magazines. Impressive, the magazines they sell. And the people who buy those magazines. The same magazines, always, with the same covers, the same articles, the same actresses, the same parties, the same diets, a totally blonde world. Brazil was now a nation of blondes, I concluded, seeing the covers of those magazines. Even our black women are blondes. Teresa was also a blonde, I noticed. She'd bleached her hair. And she looked good, the golden tone softened her expressive face, tamed her features. I was about to say, 'You look very nice,' but Teresa beat me to the punch, telling me I looked 'awful'. 'A horrible appearance.'

At a quarter of six I bought a book by Coetzee and went to the airport bar. I didn't manage to read a single line. Not even the camphor could mask the frightful smell of the carpet. I was a specialist in recognizing the smell of carpets, even after they'd been removed. The stench imprints itself on the surroundings, just as the sound produced by a good conductor remains with the orchestra. There are orchestras in which the conductor's sound is so impregnated that you need several rehearsals to get rid of it. That's the advantage of music. But with carpets there's nothing, no product, that can put an end to that damned smell.

At seven I called Marie from a payphone.

'Where are you? They said you'd left the hotel,' she said.

'On the road, headed for Liguria. I return to Naples on Sunday. What about you?'

I don't know what else we talked about, I was too upset. I only remember that she said something like: 'Cláudio is building a very good relationship with the orchestra,' and that it bothered me. 'Cláudio is an idiot,' I replied, before hanging up, although I thought otherwise; I respected my assistant.

I went back to the bar, where the waiter had turned on the television. I sat on the sofa for a long time, feeling the blood throb in my temples. And then it all began to be quite clear. It's not enough to have things, because you can lose everything at any time, any minute, everything can come to an end. That's what love is. A thing ready to end. Marie, who had been mine, no longer belonged to me, our association, our pact, she had thrown it all in the garbage. I understood the situation perfectly. Marie was betraying me. It was precisely at that moment that I came to think in those terms. Till then, what I felt was a kind of diffuse suffering; it took a time for the word to occur to me, summarizing everything, in all its force: betrayal. Better to lose her, I thought. Imagining her dead was less painful. It's funny how ideas form in men's heads. That's what I thought when I read horrible news items in the papers. Can it be, I would think, can it be that it simply happened, without planning, is it fate? Can it be that facts pile up in the future and, no matter what you do, one day they come into your life? How do tragedies happen? They happen like this: ideas suddenly pop into our heads. At first they're a thin thread, a near-nothing, and you try not to think about it, but you do think about it, all the time. Everything was crystal clear at that moment. I was full of hate. And I thought about rivals, about vows, secret things. And daggers. Knives. Poisons.

Ropes. Blows. Potassium. Where was Marie that night I phoned her? After the third whiskey everything was easy, I worked out a definitive solution to my problem, a perfect way to feel no pain of any kind. But then everything disappeared and I fell asleep.

I woke up in the bar at 10:15 at night, with lots of noise around me. I felt dizzy. I thought of going to Teresa's, maybe that was better. Maybe it was safer. For a few minutes I missed my old life with her, our tranquility. I still remembered the pleasure of picking up an unfamiliar score, sitting at the piano in our living room, a cup of coffee in my hand, being there, without haste, imagining my orchestra that I knew so well, foreseeing each solo, and Teresa on the sofa, making everything so calm. I missed going home and burying my nose in Teresa's short-cut hair before going to sleep, sharing silence with Teresa, on Sunday, the two of us reading the papers. But this lasted only a brief time, I imagined getting myself there, and the desire to return simply vanished.

I took a taxi. It was raining heavily. The wet asphalt, reflecting the lights of the city, made it seem less sordid. But that was just an impression. São Paulo was still rotting.

I asked the driver to stop at the corner of the block. I got out, walked down the street, dragging my wheeled luggage. There were others doing the same, only with their dogs. At least, I thought, suitcases don't defecate.

At ten minutes past midnight I stood at the door to my apartment. I was trembling. I was afraid, but not exactly of what I would find inside. It was fear of myself. I put the key in the lock and went inside.

12

IT WAS A POINTED shoe of delicate leather in a burnt-reddish tone, lined with pale pink silk, and the name Valentino in bas-relief. Above, three tiny roses, handmade. 'I think these are the loveliest shoes I've ever had,' Marie had said when she received them as a gift from her mother. On her slim feet they were like jewels, and there in my hand they seemed a kind of trophy that I would never be worthy of receiving. I've lost, I thought.

Shortly after meeting Marie, I had come to the conclusion that it wasn't at all hard to live with a woman thirty years younger. Basically, it just requires you to fake it all the time. And we maestros know how to fake it. There is no other profession in which one can fake it as much. Fake enthusiasm, vigor. Efficiency. Erudition. Power. Success. Virility. I can't explain the phenomenon in other terms, but the sexual attraction that a conductor arouses has a lot to do with it. 'Women like conductors,' my conducting professor used to say in Germany. 'When we step onto the podium, baton in hand, they hear what Chopin shouted to Delfina Potocka: "God save the omnipotent penis!"'

But, in the end, I hadn't faked it enough, I thought, placing the shoe on the floor.

I moved around, very carefully, observing details, my

study, my piano, my Brahms on the wall, my books; my things were all there, but it was as if nothing really worked. It was no longer my house. Newspapers scattered about, scores, everything wrong. I felt agitated, thought about leaving, going to a hotel, but instead I went to the kitchen and got a sashimi knife we'd bought in New York.

I wandered around a bit before going to our bedroom and standing at the door, without moving, feeling an icy current rising quickly inside me, which seemed to spring from the blade. I tried to listen to what was going on inside the bedroom, but there was a buzzing in my head, like a machine, a running motor, that wouldn't let me hear anything.

I felt myself being invaded by a swarm of horrible thoughts.

I opened the door, and this is what I saw: the television on, and Marie sleeping in our bed, in panties and a T-shirt, hugging a book.

I turned on the lights and began ransacking the room. Marie sat up, startled, not knowing what was happening. 'Where is he?' I asked, while rummaging through closets, drawers, and throwing everything on the floor.

Her stupefied air irritated me. Sitting on the edge of the bed, her hair in disarray; suddenly there was no beauty left in Marie. A quite common type, totally without attraction, she seemed like a faded doll, disjointed, unable to utter a sound besides huh and shh and sobs. Even her fragility exasperated me at that moment.

Marie tried to leave the bedroom, but I was faster and stood in front of the door.

'Do you know who I am?'

She remained silent, and her eyes bulged, making me really crazy. When things go bad, women turn into victims.

They commit enormous acts of stupidity, they betray, they deceive, lie, embitter, fuck everything, and when there's no way out, they start to cry.

'I know everything there is to know about lying and deceiving,' I said. Marie was crying, but that scene didn't work with me. I went on telling her that I was the maestro and that I knew everything that was going on in that house, the conspiracy, I knew there was someone inside there trying to destroy me, but I was strong and I had a knife. 'Nobody's going to take my place,' I shouted. I didn't want to say all those things, but I was powerless to stop myself. I got lost in the sentences, lost my train of thought, everything became a jumble inside me. I spoke of a plot involving high-ranking people. And that she had spent the night away with some enemy of mine. That she had betrayed me. Screwed lots of men. That my heart was torn apart. That I loved her. And that Mahler had said that where there's music there too is the devil. I said she was just 'a string player', and that strings were the middle class of the orchestra, the pediatricians and dentists and schoolteachers of music, who were constantly frustrated because they never succeeded in becoming soloists and remained there in their pitiful little middle-class lives, contributing their mediocre little bit. And that she wasn't even a viola, if she were at least a viola she could consider herself an aristocrat and look down on the strings the way Marie Antoinette looked down on the starving rabble. And that she should hang out with the trumpets and trombones, our proletarians, uncultured, gross people, excellent hod carriers.

Afterward, Marie told me that I grabbed her by the hair and made her kneel and look under the bed with me. I don't remember doing that. But I do remember pointing the knife at her. I also remember the sensation of terror that suddenly gripped me when I noticed that weapon between us. It was a sensation that made me hand her the knife.

'Use this piece of crap,' I shouted, as Marie tried to escape from me and I tried to force the knife into her hands.

This happened after I had turned the bedroom upside down and thrown everything onto the floor, including Marie's violin. The thought came to me that she was hiding something inside the instrument, proof, papers. I tore up everything.

I heard Marie leave. I could have run after her, but I decided to finish my search. I ransacked the entire place, there was nothing anywhere, in the drawers, the closets, underneath the furniture, behind the pictures, in the luggage storage area, or the shoeboxes. On the soap in the bathroom, not a single hair. The only thing I found were piles of newspapers with news about Israel, under our bed. Most of them spoke of bombs going off and showed photos of people bleeding and soldiers at work in the rescue effort. I read almost everything. The problem for the doctors in Gaza is the cases of drop foot, the papers said. The Palestinians send the children to throw stones at Israeli soldiers, who respond by shooting at the urchins' legs. Suicide bomber kills nineteen in Israel. Suicide terrorist kills fourteen in Israel. Seventeen dead, ninety-nine injured. Black Friday: forty-five dead. In Ramallah, 150 tanks occupied the city. Snipers were everywhere. That's what was in the newspapers. I don't know how Marie could still think of peace with the Palestinians. She'd told me that – that she still believed in peace. That it was really all a question of dividing the land and setting up two states. Peace. I laughed when I recalled that. And then I sank to the floor, without the strength even to walk.

I crawled to the living room and spent the rest of the night awake, thinking. First, I was overcome by a great sense of relief; after all, it was good that Marie had left, that everything had ended this way. At last I was free of it all. Free of that hell. Of doubt. Of the newspapers beneath the bed, filled with blood and hatred. In time, I thought, I'd forget Marie. And I wouldn't be losing all that much. For I had never, at any moment, succeeded in possessing her completely. Our happiness had always been shaky. Always fleeting, temporary. As soon as I entered her body, she was no longer there. And when I withdrew, she returned. And shut me out. In and out and it's all over, that's what loving Marie was. Much better to end it, I thought. Maybe I'd even go back to Teresa. I even phoned my ex-wife, but Eduarda said she wasn't home yet. Two in the morning and she was still in the street. That had to end too. Teresa and her ridiculous behavior. Those too-tight clothes, and now she was a blonde. With absolutely no wrinkles. When we separated, Teresa was nothing but wrinkles, and now, magically, the wrinkles were gone. A farce. And now I was frec. I would totally forget the hell of my marriages. My work would help me. I had music. Music above all else.

Throughout the night, I felt relieved. Later, when morning came, I was assailed by a great feeling of guilt. Only then did I see clearly what had happened. I was poisoned. Maybe by something I'd eaten on the plane. There was a steel ball in my stomach. My neck was stiff. My arms ached. Maybe it was some kind of illness. Maybe I should see a doctor. Maybe there was something that could block the whole process. That way, with it blocked, I could be happy with Marie. We would stay at the point at which I was crazy about her and she about me.

Thinking these thoughts brought me peace. I had food

poisoning, that's what I'd tell Marie. I looked around for pills, there were some in the bathroom. I fell asleep leaning against the tub, with the sensation that everything was all but resolved. It was just a matter of adjustment.

13

A NURSE AND A needle pricking my arm, that was the first thing I saw. Only afterward did I detect Marie's scent. I saw her hair. Her face was a blur, I couldn't make out her features. Monique was beside her, saying things in her mezzo-soprano voice. Maybe she was talking to me. 'She has a pretty voice,' I said. I felt a little groggy, and it took me a while to understand what was happening. Gradually, my sight returned to normal. I asked them all to leave. Marie remained at my side, and explained that the day after I arrived in Brazil, Jânia, our maid, had found me on the floor in the bathroom. I had taken a massive dose of sleeping pills and had twice suffered cardiac arrest, just after getting to the hospital. I'd been in the ICU for several days and was out of danger now.

We're so afraid of dying, we spend our entire lives fearing our end, suffering over the idea of nothingness, and the only thing I could say about nearly dying was that there's no momentum in death. In that sense, it's very anticlimactic. I didn't remember anything, not even having wanted to die, if in fact that's what I wanted. You stop feeling, it's over; that's what dying is.

Everything struck me as good those days. Marie zealously looked after my health, perhaps because she felt responsible for what had happened. It had its amusing side, observing the awkwardness of the people around me; they all felt uncomfortable with a suicide, they didn't know what to say to me, much less how to conceal what they knew about my act of desperation. Besides that, a failed suicide is not only a convalescent, he's also a kind of hero, looked upon with a certain degree of admiration; after all, it's not everyone who tries to kill himself. Try putting a bullet into your own chest. At the hospital, they paid no attention to the fact that I was famous. What really gave me status was my suicidal gesture. The truth is that suicides comprise the artistic class of the world of pathologies. You perceive everything in the people who come into contact with you, compassion, curiosity, and even the desire to ask for an autograph and advice. If at that moment I had wanted to start a brotherhood of suicides, it wouldn't have been difficult. When I sat in the garden to get some sun, those undergoing treatment for depression would show up by the handful for idle talk about music, then quickly get to the point: perfect techniques for killing oneself. One lady told me: 'One day we'll get there.' She had already tried twice. 'Sleeping pills aren't any good,' she concluded. 'Strychnine is better.'

Only the rabble treat us with disdain. When they come to clean our room, they feel a great sense of superiority and look at us as if we were demons, and it has to do with what's taught in churches about altruism and acceptance. If death is easy, what's hard is to go on mopping floors and wallowing in the godforsaken outskirts. What's hard is raising a child and washing dirty clothes. That's what's hard, the cleaning ladies seemed to be telling me.

In short, there's nothing like a near-suicide. 'The maestro is resting,' Marie would say when they phoned from the orchestra, 'the maestro can't be disturbed.' Of course I enjoyed it. We maestros love being treated like that. My professor of conducting, in Germany, was so used to that ceremonious treatment that he ended up referring to himself in the third person. 'The maestro wants you to be careful with your impulses,' he told me right away in the first class. 'What maestro?' I asked, still unaware of his idiosyncrasies. Ingenuously, I thought there was a higher 'maestro', a kind of god to whom we should address ourselves, and who would be the supreme judge of our final exam. 'Is there another one in the room?' my master replied. 'I'm the maestro. The only one.' In the beginning I found his eccentricity amusing, but some years later, when I was out in the world conducting the orchestras we have to conduct, during that phase of life when we're neither talented young conductors nor wise old conductors, when we're in the limbo of our profession, that age bracket from thirty to fifty, conducting whatever they put in front of us, I understood why our craft is so revered. It's a form of payment. There's nothing more lonely than the life of a conductor. As has already been said, we're always between a rock and a hard place, between the musicians and the public, between the score and the interpretation. In addition, music no longer has any meaning in the modern world. Classical music is for the few. It always has been. The same is the case with opera. Before it became popular, in Italy, it was the art of the court, of lovers of Greek tragedy, and history buffs. We continue to be as elitist as in the seventeenth century. Only more isolated, without prestige, almost useless. It's a profession whose days are numbered, some predict. Therefore we're treated with the same reverence as the golden lion monkey and other species on the verge of extinction.

'I don't want to be king or emperor,' Wagner said, 'maestro is enough for me.' It took Marie some time to understand that. It was necessary for me to almost die.

Teresa, I recall, had been much quicker. But then too, after the separation her attitude changed radically. She never again said, 'Bring the maestro some coffee,' as was her custom. It became 'he'. 'See if "he" wants coffee,' she would say when I visited Eduarda. But Marie, there in the hospital, started treating me with deference. At first she only referred to me that way when doctors or nurses were in the room, and later, as a joke, she started doing so when we were alone. 'I'm dying to suck your dick, maestro.'

Anyway, I regained my peace in the hospital. I loved the smell of alcohol that overpowered the other odors, and the smell of sterilized linen; only the smell of food was bothersome, but that ceased once they brought me my camphor. Sometimes, because of the medication, I felt like a sack of potatoes lying in bed, but even that was a good sensation.

We were totally at peace, Marie and I. We didn't speak about what had taken place, the knife, my jealousy, the shattered violin. It was as if nothing had happened. We didn't comment on the incident even when Marie brought to the hospital the new violin her parents had given her. We spent the afternoon enraptured by the beauty of the instrument, and when she played passages of a Brahms concerto, I exaggeratedly pointed out the quality of its harmonics, although they weren't all that different from those of the old violin that I had smashed.

As for the two of us, it sometimes occurred to me that the crisis had brought us closer together. It's difficult to explain our process, but it was a game. Marie had invented the game. She would begin by provoking me. I would react, she would punish me. Part of the game was that it had to be my fault. Always. I would get desperate, she would be amused. It was also part of the game that if I wanted to end the tension, I had to exaggerate, imploring, shouting, causing a scandal, and then Marie would draw back. Everything would return to normal. Now, we were at the point where one would kill himself for the other, and that's why she was so happy at the hospital. The suicide was the high point of our romance. A wonderful life, there in the hospital. She would arrive early, with the newspapers, get in bed with me, and we'd read together. In the afternoon we strolled through the gardens or the corridors, holding hands, taking it easy. At times I would study a score while she read, calmly, lying on the sofa. We also watched a lot of films, videotapes that she brought from the rental place near our home. We had espresso sent up from the bar, to drink with the chocolates that visitors brought me. 'The good part of being a convalescent is that you can do things without feeling the least bit guilty,' said Marie. 'It's only through marijuana that I've managed to have the freedom of the convalescent. Until I started smoking marijuana, I never knew what it was to spend the afternoon in bed without feeling a certain unease. If I wasn't studying, I felt guilty. Sometimes I would just grip the violin, paralyzed, I couldn't concentrate enough to study or find the peace to do anything else. See a movie, for example. What's wrong with going to a matinee? I went back to Dalva, the black woman who raised me, who introjected in me the notion of Kantian duty. She was an old-school Protestant. My parents were always traveling, and Dalva was responsible for my upbringing. And for Dalva, upbringing meant having a schedule for everything. You have no idea what my routine was. A time for eating, for watching TV, for doing homework, for sleeping, for waking up. And when my mother would come back from a trip, the two of them would argue because of Dalva's severity, but Dalva always won. She would threaten to quit, and my mother always gave in. I had an enormous fear of repeating a year. Dalva talked about "repeaters" as if they were lepers. Dalva was hell on wheels. The truth is, because of that I started smoking marijuana. Marijuana did for me what seven years of therapy couldn't. I got free of Dalva. You ought to smoke too. Marijuana allows me to do nothing. To not have schedules. To plop down on the sofa without reading, without studying, no obligations. To go to the corner for ice cream. To sit on a park bench and stay there, watching, without rushing, the bums, the nannies, the pigeons, the popcorn vendors. To turn on the television and watch all that crap. Life is that too. I'm going to roll a joint for you one of these days.'

At night we would turn on CNN and follow the movements of the Israeli army. Marie had become a specialist on the subject, and knew details such as the Palestinian GDP pre- and post-Intifada, as well as the names of the Hamas and Islamic Jihad suicide bombers.

'And what about our violence?' I once asked.

'How so?'

'You're so interested in violence, so why not take a look at our war? I don't understand how, being Brazilian, you only manage to truly suffer when the Arabs throw stones at Jewish children. Why don't you look at our newspapers?'

'It's different. It's not a war.'

'It's worse than your war. You have an ideal.'

On such occasions, Marie would give me lessons on what it meant to be Jewish, the significance of a conflict that had already lasted for close to a century, the creation of the state of Israel, and related issues. I felt uncomfortable with those conversations. It was as if she were telling me: you're a goy. I'm a Jew. That pain, that expectation, that desire are mine and you'll never understand them. 'You don't understand,' the whole family would tell me. Mira, Marie's grandmother, the only time she visited me, related a lengthy story about her trip to Jerusalem when Israel had won the Six Day War. 'It was only a week after the war ended, Jews were coming from all over, desperate to get to the Wall. I felt as if I were taking part in one of the pilgrimages that happened a thousand years ago, with Jews going to visit the holy temple. Just the memory of it gives me chills. You don't know what it's like,' she said. 'I can imagine,' I replied, out of politeness. 'No, no, you can't,' she contradicted me. 'You have to be Jewish to understand.'

Visits, reading, TV, that's how we spent the days. I felt better and better. My psychiatrist talked to Marie and me, advising me to undergo analysis: 'The medicine helps,' he said, 'but therapeutic backup is essential.'

'I'm not going to do that,' I told Marie.

'Are you afraid to?'

'Laziness. Laziness about talking.'

'But it's medical assistance.'

'You sound like Monique when you say "medical assistance". Marie, my lovely, my princess, I believe in medicine. Fresh fish stinks.'

'I'm not following your reasoning. Help me out.'

'Brodsky and I have a theory. Psychoanalysis thaws the fish. And psychiatry keeps the fish smelling good.'

Marie laughed. Then she went to the phone and set up an appointment with Dr. Homero for the following week.

Adriana visited me the day I was released. Something had come out in a newspaper about my being in the hospital, and some reporters had phoned, asking for details.

'If it's to write about Strauss's *Domestic Symphony*, those fuckers are as slow as the devil, but when it's to find out if you really tried to kill yourself –' Suddenly, Adriana stopped short. She looked at me for a few seconds.

'Go on,' I said.

'I don't believe you tried to kill yourself.'

'Is that what the reporters wanted to know?'

'I don't know where they got that from. You wouldn't kill yourself. I know how suicides work.'

'What became of your boyfriend?'

'He went away. Want me to finish my theory?'

'What theory?'

'About suicides.'

'Go ahead.'

'You're not happy, anybody can see that. To be happy, you've got to have an automatic idiot. Know what that is? You go to the mirror and say, OK, everything's all right. You fuck yourself, go to Alcoholics Anonymous, almost die from trying to stop drinking, but you say, OK, I'm happy. You lose your boyfriend and say, fine, I'm not going to kill myself. That's not how it is with you. You're very anguished, you suffer all day long. I've known that ever since I came to the orchestra. You suffer a lot, we can see that. But you're also not the kind who kills himself.'

'No?'

'Not suicide. You're more the homicidal type. Speaking of which, did you see the São Paulo game yesterday?'

Marie didn't like Adriana. 'Why do you two laugh so much? I go out and you're laughing. I come back, you're still laughing. What's so funny?'

It was Adriana who laughed. I just listened. Above all, Marie picked on my secretary's choice of clothes.

'She definitely doesn't know what's a nice blouse tucked into long pants. I've never seen Adriana in jeans. It's just short skirts and a top, she's always rubbing that piercing of hers in our faces. Besides which, that passion for football is a total lie. Grandstanding. She's trying to impress you.'

I left the hospital on a Friday afternoon. Returning home, by Rua da Consolação, in a rainstorm, with the traffic completely stalled, I could think only that I loved the city, I loved Marie, loved my work, my orchestra, and that it had nothing to do with the automatic idiot. Everything was going well, everything was calm, the outlook was good. And I was dying to get back to the orchestra and set up our next football game.

14

'HAVE YOU SEEN OUR MOSQUES? They did away with them. Those murderers did not spare even the Church of the Nativity. Only destruction is what you will find here. Our children are being killed cruelly,' said a Palestinian. The testimony of an Israeli: 'We're sick of that cynicism. We do not destroy churches.' When I came into the living room, trying to avoid Jânia, Marie was in front of the TV, watching the news, seeing images of attacks on hotels and restaurants.

'Stay here with me,' she said.

I lay down beside her. Marie tousled my hair as the newscast ran a story about the discovery of manuals for terrorists containing recipes for nitroglycerin and ammonium nitrate, in Jordan.

I didn't take my eyes off the hall, always tuned to Jânia's movements. I had the sensation that she was constantly in motion, maybe spying on us.

'Aren't you going to study anymore?' Marie asked.

I pretended to be interested in the newscast. I didn't want to be by myself in the study. Ever since returning from the hospital, I'd had the impression that Jânia was following me around the house, waiting for an opportunity to be alone with me. As soon as I arrived, she greeted me at the door, squeezing my hands with enough force to change a tire. I didn't like it one bit. And minutes before, that night, I was alone in my study, wrestling with Lutoslawski's *Concerto for Orchestra*, which I was to conduct soon, a work full of technical and structural difficulties that demanded tremendous concentration on my part, when I heard her rubber slippers shuffling through the hall. A horrible sensation took hold of me, despite my having no reason to fear or avoid Jânia, except for a certain discomfort at having previously asked her to keep watch over Marie. But that had been resolved. I'd told her plainly that I didn't want to know anything. The problem was that Jânia was behaving strangely. No matter what I told her, whether to iron a shirt or pick up a package left with the doorman, she would simply smile, a smile that might signify acceptance, indifference, or menace. That night, she appeared at the door of the study and gestured to me. True, she might have been merely saying goodnight, but I could have sworn she was beckoning me to join her in a private conversation. That's what I perceived. Come, she said. I didn't go, of course. But I had a sense of imminent tragedy, as if she were about to tell me something terrible. The very sight of Jânia put me on guard, expecting danger.

I slept badly that night. There was a party going on in the building, and the sound of the music woke me several times. I tossed and turned for much of the time, watching the hours pass, restless, with awful foreboding. I kept getting up to check that the windows were closed.

The next morning, I asked Marie to find a way to keep Jânia from coming into the living room while we were having breakfast.

'Why?'

'She's watching us,' I said.

'Jânia? Jânia adores me.'

Marie's self-esteem was something that had impressed me from the beginning. The cook adored her. The doorman at the orchestra adored her. The parking valet. The bar owner. Marie took a special pleasure in saying she was loved by the people who served her. She interpreted as adoration any manifestation of respect, cordiality, attention, or subservience. The truth is that the rich have developed various forms of dealing with their guilt; some become philanthropists, others create NGOs and foundations, and Marie was part of the class that revered the poor. She adored the rabble, and vice versa. Everybody loved her. Including Jânia.

'You're saying that she spies on us, listens to our conversations behind doors?'

'Maybe. I don't know. She's curious about us.'

'Jânia barely understands what we do for a living. Why would she spy on us? She's a poor thing.'

I said nothing. Maybe Marie was right, maybe it was just a fixation. I thought about telling her how Jânia had startled me that morning by coming into the bathroom while I was shaving. I was surprised at her image reflected in the mirror, just like in B suspense films. I had the impression that Jânia had said something to me. Or she might have been chewing gum, it's true. But I saw her lips form the word *mon-ey*. I'm not sure, but it might have been that.

I left for the orchestra very early; I had a lot to do, I'd been away for a long time and the work had piled up. I went into my room, and the problems started exploding. Even before rehearsal I had two meetings, discussed the contract for the German recording with my agent, spoke with my lawyer about royalties for the artists in the orchestra, told Adriana to set up new auditions, other meetings, and phoned Pedro Ricardo to arrange another football game.

Maybe it really was a good way to bring the musicians closer together, and our football technique hadn't yet been fully explored. Pedro Ricardo mentioned a championship that was being organized in the interior. 'Small orchestras. A few bands too.'

Adriana took the wind out of my sails. 'They don't want to play.'

'Who?' I asked.

'The musicians. Besides which, football doesn't solve the problem of our crazies. All musicians are flaky. Real wackos. We need the conventional method, electroshock, Prozac, lithium, sleep therapy, things like that. It's no good coming to us with that talk about football. The only thing that works is to get those nuts together, at a set time, and listen to their drama. Their pathetic little lives. Why don't you find a psychiatrist for all of us? I'd go for it. I'd tell my entire history to any doctor who came here. I'd grind him down with my horrible childhood and my alcoholism. I mean, provided he promised to prescribe some psychotropics. The really good ones. The type you take and bang, you're asleep. Traditional treatments are the only thing that works with us. I hope you don't have to break somebody else's scapula for Pedro Ricardo to realize that.'

The rehearsal went really badly. From my schooldays I had learned to conduct from memory. In that aspect my master was Bülow: 'You have to have the score in your head, not your head in the score.' That day, however, the music twice escaped me completely. The notes disappeared. I was going to my room, thinking about it, concerned, when Marie overtook me in the hall. She wanted to make a request in the name of the orchestra. 'They're still unhappy about what happened with Rodrigo,' she said. 'Forget about that soccer business.'

'What happened with Rodrigo?' I asked.

'You dislocated his scapula, in the game. That's why he was on leave.'

Marie complained when the musicians treated her as my spy, but apparently they didn't mind using her as their messenger girl. That got to me. Maybe I shouldn't have rehired Rodrigo, I thought.

'What's this Rodrigo business?' I asked. 'Who told you to speak to me?'

'Why are you yelling?'

'Doesn't that guy ever give up?'

'Good lord! What are you talking about?'

'About men who look at your breasts during rehearsal. Men who don't know how to play football. Men who break their scapulas and organize the musicians against me.'

Marie closed her eyes and for a moment stood there in silence, as if searching for words. 'Listen here,' she said. 'Just listen.' Pause. 'Let's agree on something.' Agitated, her hands on her waist, Marie couldn't organize what she wanted to say, she needed time to hide her indignation. In the meantime, I managed to calm down too.

'Sorry,' I said. 'Rodrigo's a cool guy.'

'You talk about him as if –' Marie stopped, sighing.

'As if –?'

'Fuck Rodrigo. Fuck the game too. I only brought it up because I thought it'd be good for you. For your relationship with the musicians.'

'There is a way you could convince me,' I said in a lively tone. Marie put her arms around my neck.

'Yeah? What happened today in the rehearsal? You weren't focused.'

'Listen to what I'm about to suggest. Let's compromise.'

'Compromise how?'

'Jânia. Fire her and I'll cancel the game.'

Marie drew back, suspicious. 'Are you OK?'

I laughed nervously. Maybe it wasn't the right moment to bring up the subject.

'What's the problem?' Marie asked.

'I don't like her.'

'Jânia's no supermaid, I admit that. She doesn't cook, she's got that dumb expression, I agree, but she's a good person. She supports her mother, she's got a bastard of a stepfather, a drunk, who's always giving her a hard time. I don't know why you've got it in for her.'

'I have a bad feeling, it's hard to explain.'

'What kind of feeling?'

'Being watched. Conspiracy. She's going to betray us.'

Marie looked at me warily. She said she couldn't understand how I could talk about a conspiracy. And about Rodrigo. She asked a lot of questions. 'Do you feel persecuted?' She wanted to know whether I was sleeping well. Whether I was taking the medication the way I should. Whether I was going regularly to the sessions with Dr. Homero.

I got a bit balled up trying to calm her. I gave a long speech about Rodrigo's expressive sound, his incredible tuning ability. 'I have nothing against him.' I also promised I'd cancel the game. 'Keep Jânia,' I said finally.

When we parted, Marie seemed quite concerned.

I went back to my room and asked Adriana to cancel the game. I spent the rest of the day studying the score. I shouldn't have spoken about conspiracy to Marie. I carefully reviewed the passages that had gotten away from me during the rehearsal. Or about Rodrigo. I had done that piece so many times, how could I have forgotten it? Now that was betrayal.

Before going home, Cláudio, my assistant, appeared in the room, somewhat nervous. There was a strange harmony between his mood and the state of his hair.

'Comb your hair,' I said.

It had been some time since we had talked personally. Cláudio had been away in the preceding months, conducting in Boston and Toronto, advancing his career outside of Brazil. We liked each other a lot, but lately he had distanced himself from me. I thought at first that it was just a matter of schedules. But that day it became clear there was something else.

'Well?' I asked.

He spoke of the trip, said the Canadian musicians played Strauss very well, that the pianist was one of those music machines who never missed a note, never raised a doubt. 'A drag,' he said, 'they played Villa-Lobos without style and without soul.' Cláudio avoided meeting my eye. He said something else about Toronto, quoted somebody or other who said that the city was Chinese with Chinese, Jew with Jew, and black with black, and further foolishness along those lines.

'Is everything all right?' I asked as he was leaving.

'The orchestra is fine. I attended your rehearsal.'

'I'm not asking about the orchestra. I'm referring to you.'

'Very well,' he said, anxious to leave the room.

'He has a lover,' Adriana told me later. Her theory was that we knew Cláudio's lover. Or he wouldn't be acting 'that way' on the telephone. 'Hi! Where are you? Can I call you in two minutes?' said Adriana, imitating Cláudio. And, she concluded, 'Only someone who has a lover talks on the phone worried about not mentioning the person's name. I know all about lovers.'

'Do you think it could be Marie?' I asked.

Adriana looked at me in surprise. 'You're not serious, I presume.'

'Of course not.'

When I got home, Jânia was still there.

'Maestro,' she said.

I pretended not to hear. I took my pills, went into the bedroom, locked the door, and waited for Marie to return.

15

IT WAS NECESSARY TO hold my breath and, in a rapid gesture, open my wallet, take out the bills and hand over the money, as if I were doing nothing. Worse, as if it were natural, a legitimate payment. A contract. As soon as Jânia appeared in front of me, I would hand her money. We said nothing, most times I didn't even look her in the eye but just put the bills on the tray, pretending to be absorbed in something.

The idea of being taken by surprise, of the moment for payoff catching me empty-handed, terrified me. I became an assiduous user of automatic teller machines and began to strategically place a few bills in pockets and the drawers of the apartment.

I still remember how Jânia's blackmail started. It was a Monday. Marie was asleep, I was having breakfast, reading about the usual horrors, homicides, skinheads and their baseball bats, the skyrocketing rates of all kinds of crap, kidnappings, Uganda – in a word, I was digesting my daily dose of tragedy before going to the orchestra, when I noted a sign from Jânia. I was totally fed up with the coded messages she was sending me. I decided to settle the matter once and for all, and sought her out in the kitchen. I found her leaning against the sink, slathering margarine on a slice of bread.

'You want to speak with me?' I asked.

I had the impression that she nodded her head, but her lips emitted a sonorous no.

I don't recall the details of that conversation, but before I realized it I was offering Jânia money. After that, our relationship became automatic. All that was necessary was for us to be alone, and I would take out my wallet and give her some money. Actually, I felt pressured to do so, as if by such action I could avoid a catastrophe.

What was most agonizing was the feeling of being tied to Jânia, as if we belonged to a terrorist group that was meeting to decide who would be the next suicide bomber. Now my house no longer signified comfort but menace, constraint. No sooner had I sat on the sofa, to read or study, than Jânia showed up to collect. It didn't matter how much I gave her, the woman always wanted more; she never tired of extorting me. And despite my insistence, Marie refused to fire her.

To avoid unpleasantness, I adopted the tactic of asking the doorman, upon entering the building, if my wife had arrived, for I'd noticed that Jânia felt inhibited by her presence. If Marie was out, I would go up to Rachel's apartment. My neighbor had gotten rid of the cast and was now walking with some difficulty, using crutches.

For some time the orchestra administration had been handling her payments and banking services, and it was common for Rachel to phone, asking me to buy some medication or other at the pharmacy. She loved medicine of every kind, she was a specialist in migraines and used expressions like 'latest generation' and 'nonresidual' when she talked about the advantages of her preferred products. I liked to visit Rachel, and I also took her to my concerts, where she sat in my box. 'I'm going to tell you something: you look lovely onstage. You look like an actor. You know I'd never noticed your air of a leading man?' We were sitting in the kitchen, she was making coffee, we were eating bread with butter, and I was listening to her harp on the same old subject, how stupid her daughter's life was. 'She's very well paid, no two ways about that. And she has status too. She's always around those people from the IMF, that whole pack of economists. But I keep thinking, maestro, is it normal for anybody to live like that, stuck inside a bank all year long, without seeing the sky, without a husband, boyfriend, vacation, children, a dog, nothing? A woman who doesn't even have time to love a man? The feminists can say whatever they want, but there comes a time when nothing in our lives is more important than motherhood. True enough, later on you get yourself in a fine pickle. You dream that you'll always have the love of your children, that the little baby who waves his arms in joy when he sees you will be incapable of abandoning you. And then what happens? You end up a widow, and they don't care one iota about how lonely you are.' After a pause: 'She hasn't called me for two weeks. I mean, two weeks and two days.'

In a frame in the living room was a photo of Esther that aroused my curiosity. A suit, intelligent gaze, an interesting woman. She must do well with the cabinet ministers. 'The truth is,' Rachel said at the end of our conversation, 'my daughter doesn't like me.'

Marie didn't like Rachel either, 'that old chatterbox of a woman,' she said, and Rachel really did talk too much, but there was something in her chattering, or in her house, with its old somber-colored furniture, that soothed me. Sometimes I would fall asleep in the armchair and Marie would have to come herself and wake me, because Rachel refused to disturb me.

Anyway. What matters is that when I returned from one of my frequent visits to Rachel I found Jânia and Marie in the kitchen. They interrupted their conversation when they noticed me. I panicked. Get that woman out of here, I thought. Marie was quicker, she asked me to give them a few minutes by themselves. I waited in the hallway and listened as Jânia recounted the problems she faced at her mother's, where her stepfather harassed her every night, threatening her. To my amazement, Marie settled the matter in two seconds, by inviting her to live with us. There was a good maid's room, with its own bath, and she could stay there, no problem. 'If the maestro doesn't mind,' Marie concluded.

'I don't want that girl living here,' I told Marie as she went into the bathroom to brush her teeth. 'It's all a lie,' I said, from the bedroom. 'I doubt very much that anyone wants to see her pussy.'

Marie came to the door, as if wanting to be certain that I had uttered that vulgarity. After rinsing her mouth and washing her face, she returned to the bedroom and asked whether I didn't feel any compassion. She went on at length about what was worrying her, Jânia's fragility, the possibility of an unwanted pregnancy, the grave consequences of such an occurrence for the family.

I didn't give in.

'It's just for a while,' Marie insisted. 'I promise.'

'They like that kind of confusion.'

'They who?'

'Them,' I replied.

'Them. Of course. The poor. The rabble, right? They, the riffraff, as you put it. The hordes. The trash.'

Enraged, Marie stated that 'the rabble are the only good thing in this country', and that, 'for that matter', she 'hated' that way I had of alluding to the 'more humble', that the fact of my using the word *rabble* showed how much I despised 'the people', and that Jânia was a high-quality 'human asset'.

'I fully agree,' I said. 'She's better than all the tenors put together.'

Marie didn't laugh at my comment; she immediately said that in that aspect I was precisely 'a maestro'. Great, I thought. It begins. She was already like my old lovers, who at the beginning of the relationship loved me because I was a maestro and later, when not everything turned out as they would like, hated me for being a maestro.

Marie's harangue continued, full blast. I was surprised to learn that she detested 'the dark side' of my personality, that 'damnable sense of superiority so common in conductors'. I listened to her criticisms attentively and with all seriousness, but when she started accusing me of being 'anti-North-easterner' and saying that I despised popular culture, folk-lore, that I detested 'intelligent rock', it struck me as so ludicrous that I couldn't hold back my laughter. 'Long live the Indians,' I shouted.

Marie, completely without humor, told me that Jânia was coming to live with us. It was decided.

I was desperate. There was nowhere in the house that I felt safe. Jânia, with her short legs and her hidden plans, could catch me at any moment. I started having insomnia. Because of these episodes, Homero, my shrink, decided to change my medication. 'This story increases my suspicions. From the beginning, your case didn't strike me as depressive. I think what you suffer from is an obsessive disturbance. These bad thoughts that plague you, which psychiatry terms "intrusive", are generating a sense of being watched, pursued. I had a long conversation with Marie. Jânia appears to have no motive for acting the way you describe her. It's my view that you yourself are creating the situation.'

'She's blackmailing me.'

'How?'

I told him the whole story.

'But does she ask you for money? Does she threaten you?'

'Not verbally. But I know it's blackmail. She looks at me in a threatening manner.'

'After you give her money, how do you feel?'

'Relieved.'

'Do you ever meet with Jânia without offering her money?'

'I've never tried. She forces me to do it.'

Homero convinced me that my attitude was a compulsion, a way I had found to free myself from a discomfort of my own making.

We did in fact go with a different medicine, and within a few weeks the changes were visible. I no longer felt compelled to offer Jânia money and didn't even think about it. Actually, I couldn't think about anything. Or keep an erection, or study, or anything. The pills truly do away with our torments, but they drain the vitality out of life. We become totally dry.

It became clear that the treatment wasn't working in the middle of the following week, at the final rehearsal of *Rites of Spring*. I knew the work, its aggressive instrumentation, its constantly changing rhythms; after all, I had conducted the piece in Berne and Geneva and considered it easy and simple like few others. The last two rehearsals had been quite good, which worried me. Excellent rehearsals, mediocre concerts. Satisfied musicians are always a problem. As soon as I began the general rehearsal, I had the feeling that I was surfing a huge wave whose purpose was to devour my memory. It was as if I were racing away from forgetting by accelerating the rhythms, running. Then, at a certain moment, exhausted, I was engulfed by the wave. I felt empty, confused. I led everyone away from the central motif and created indescribable chaos. The musicians stopped playing and looked at me in surprise. Total silence in the room.

That night, I threw out all the pills. I called Homero and told him I didn't want any more of that crap. I couldn't even screw anymore because of them. My dick just wouldn't get hard. 'I tell my patients not to read the information that comes with the medicine. They get influenced and think they're susceptible to every possible side effect. Medications like this one may reduce libido. But you've only been on it for a short time. I don't think it's likely that it's affecting your memory. Or your sex life.'

'Look at that,' Marie would say when we went to bed, before the pills, 'all I have to do is put my tongue in your mouth and your dick blows up like an air bag.' She took pride in seeing her power over me. 'You can barely feel my breath,' she'd say, 'just look,' she'd say, with her hand on my penis, verifying the transformation. But the medicine put an end to that. I felt worn out, empty, without desire. 'Sexual dysfunction including impotence and ejaculatory disorders,' that was what it said in the insert.

The night before, I had been very depressed. I came home and Marie looked pretty, wearing a short black skirt and a white silk blouse. She got her purse, 'Don't even close the door,' she said, 'we're going out. You need to get away from this work-home regimen. I bought tickets to the Scorsese film.' Everything went very well. I felt up for it, in love, calm. After the movies, we went to eat at an Italian cantina. Marie drank more than usual, and we laughed a lot. We returned home, and on the way Marie told me she was happy with me. In recent days everything had been going well between us. It was good to end the day knowing she was waiting for me. Marie wasn't a good cook, and she wasn't very fond of cooking, but she did make delicious salads with Parma ham and figs, and others of that kind, light things that we would eat together before watching a DVD or reading in bed, studying – in short, it was a good moment in our lives. But that night, when we went to bed, full of desire, I couldn't get it up. I had often failed to get it up, it happens to all men, but now I knew it had to do with the pills. I showed Marie the insert. 'What good is it for me to feel good, maintain my equilibrium, if my dick is limp?' I asked. 'I've got to throw all that junk in the garbage.'

'You're tired,' she said. 'Come and lie down here with me. It's good like this, holding you, touching each other. Lie down here.'

I didn't give up. I locked myself in the bathroom and flogged my dick, thinking about everything, Marie's pussy, her wonderful ass, our sexual games, but nothing made my dick get hard. I went back to bed shattered; Marie was in a deep sleep.

And the next day the tragedy at the rehearsal proved my theory. Those pills were killing me. I couldn't screw anymore, and now I couldn't conduct either.

Although Homero insisted that suspending the medicine didn't act automatically on the system, all I can say is that because I got rid of the medication the concert that week was very good. Conducting, like creating, has to do with fury, with will, and with a stiff prick too. I conducted as in the old days, with confidence and pleasure.

On Monday, the blackmailer came to get money out of me as soon as I woke up. I didn't even let her say good morning. I had spoken with my accountant on Friday and prepared all the paperwork and money.

'You're fired,' I said.

Jânia smiled that disgusting smile at me. Perhaps she was challenging me.

'Try,' I said, 'to get one more cent out of me and it'll be the last thing you ever do.'

16

THERE WAS A TIME when if a soloist canceled a concert I would become a menace to society. That was at the very beginning, when I took over the orchestra and was obliged to explain to my Swiss agent that São Paulo, Bolivia and Uruguay were different places. But things had changed greatly since then. Actually, it wasn't at all hard to replace a violinist who had canceled a concert. Another one. Lately, cancellations seemed to be in vogue. I spent two hours on the phone with Hannah, and I could take my pick. 'Nowadays, guest artists don't ask me just about violence, string bikinis and dengue,' Hannah told me, 'they're also interested in your orchestra.'

We invited Enrique Lamadrid, an exceptionally talented musician, who was going through 'a difficult moment', according to Hannah, because of his recent separation. He'd been dumped for a motor scooter dealer, I later learned.

Lamadrid arrived in São Paulo on Monday, and Adriana, immediately after picking him up at the airport, called me, worried. 'I think you ought to be on the alert with this guy. I think he might kill himself at the hotel,' she said. That same day, I invited him to dinner at my house. It can't be easy to be dumped for a scooter dealer. I recalled Lamadrid's ex-wife, an architect, a reader of poetry, a very interesting woman. Ending up like that, with a scooter dealer? How could it have happened? There couldn't be too many scooter dealers in Barcelona. That's how women are, I thought upon seeing Lamadrid's dead-calf eyes. The best ones, like Carmen, the most talented, the most delectable, always end up with the pizza deliveryman. They need a servile attention that we cerebral types are unable to offer. We're too busy studying, creating, or making money. And then a scooter dealer comes along and, wham, game over.

Lamadrid certainly wasn't the same seductive, leading-man type I'd met years before in London. Of the old Lamadrid only the staring eyes remained, that and nothing more. As for the rest, he was a scrap of a man, filled with pain. After two shots of whiskey, he presented a quasi-scientific theory about the human being's biological tendency toward betrayal, which he'd read in one of those weekly magazines. 'A stiff prick represents the pumping of blood. Even to cheat, the male works harder. But women don't need anything. They spread their legs and problem solved.' To him, the idea of fidelity was 'a patent fallacy'. 'Scientists tell us that even fleas cheat.'

Perhaps that scientific discourse consoled Lamadrid.

'What happened with Carmen?' I asked. There was a moment of silence. Lamadrid lowered his gaze, like a lassoed cow. A sordid spectacle, complete with miserable details, would have ensued if Marie hadn't come into the room, her skin glistening beneath her colorful exercise outfit. At the same instant, the deserted misogynist was transformed into a being whose sole function was to sing the praises of my wife. I was flabbergasted by the metamorphosis. As if by magic, the corpse was transformed into a slim figure with very black hair and very white skin, elegant gestures and pointed ears, like the devil. Behold the violinist, I thought. Diabolical, seductive, roping Marie into a long conversation about violins, brimming with little laughs and gallantries that bored into my ears and clamped onto my nerves.

That night, because of the wine, Marie fell asleep in less than a minute, but I tossed in bed, seething with rage, without anything to do, with Mignone's music, which I had studied during the afternoon, echoing perfectly in my head like a wild beast. Why was I so angry at Marie, when it was the corpse who had aimed his charm at my wife? Lamadrid was a real sonofabitch. Carmen had been right to trade him for a scooter. 'Marie is the only one at the table who knows how to eat,' he said, praising the fact that my wife didn't devour, like him, the pasta dish I myself had made. The violinist's idiotic jargon was a hit with Marie. The two were enjoying themselves. Lamadrid's guffaws cantered into my brain, causing me to conjure up excruciating things.

In the midst of this agony, I felt Marie, nude, putting her legs between mine. It was like a pleasurable stabbing, a wave of electricity that shot through my body and set everything on fire. Finally I was going back to what I was. I dashed to the mirror in the bathroom and stood there looking at myself for several minutes, euphoric, how great it was to have my stiff prick back. In the final analysis, what is a man without it? What good are memory and talent if we can't get it up? I returned to the bed, Marie encircled me with her arms, sleepily, and while we made love I managed to think about that and nothing else: having a really stiff prick is a good thing.

We had a peaceful morning: we ate breakfast, I helped Marie wash the dishes, and we straightened up the house. We'd been without a maid for several days. Marie was still trying to convince me to rehire Jânia, we had even argued over it, but I was unwilling to yield. 'Let's go for a time without anyone,' I said.

When we went to the newsstand to buy a paper, I asked what she had thought about Lamadrid.

'A bore. He talks too much and thinks he's hot shit.'

We returned home holding hands. I felt calmer; there was no reason to fear the Spaniard.

On the way to the theater we spoke about the possibility of a trip to Israel. The suggestion had been mine, but Marie was unenthusiastic. 'I don't know if I'd like to go back there now,' she said. 'My girlfriends gave me a manual when I arrived in Jerusalem. Avoid crowds. Avoid buses. Buy anything you can by telephone. At the time, all the stores were offering purchases by phone and home delivery. Now, everything must be worse. And it's going to continue to be awful as long as Sharon is in power.' We agreed to go to Greece, and that I'd check my schedule so we could arrange our vacation.

To summarize, we were at peace.

Imagine then my surprise at seeing, shortly afterward, that Marie wasn't at her place for our rehearsal when I came onstage. Nor was Lamadrid. The two came in four minutes late, Lamadrid without a vestige of suicidal depression, and Marie claiming that she'd been showing the violinist around the building. I had given her oceanic orgasms all night long, my dick was raw from so much fucking, and she offered to show that vulture around? My stomach started churning when I noticed that Lamadrid was carrying Marie's violin case. 'A bore,' she'd said. But there she was, pampering the guy.

The next few days were difficult. Lamadrid was endowed with extraordinary technical skill as a violinist, but that wasn't the only reason for his popularity with my orchestra.

The musicians were literally enchanted by that Spanish head of hair. Or rather, by that forelock. All that could be seen, when he played, was that enormous forelock, which did everything but talk. It was almost a being, the forelock. After the rehearsals, the musicians stamped their feet to compliment the forelock, and I could barely conceal my irritation. Was it just an impression, or were he and Marie exchanging glances? 'Attack together,' I shouted, without succeeding in getting the violins to play in unison. They did everything wrong, the imbeciles, and I kept saying how dissatisfied I was. 'You're terrible,' I said. Cruelly, I made some of the violinists play individually. Marie was the one most criticized.

Other episodes aroused my suspicions. During a rehearsal break I saw the two of them in the cafeteria, talking. I also saw Marie lend him our guide to restaurants in São Paulo. At home, she was glued to her cell phone, even taking it into the bathroom. In some of the calls she spoke laconically, as lovers do, and, one Tuesday night, she simply disappeared, getting home at eleven o'clock. 'I told you it was Uncle Moisés's birthday,' she said. 'I came into the room when you were meeting with the producers just to say so.' She had in fact come into the room, but I didn't remember anything about Uncle Moisés. Actually, I'd never before heard mention of him. And why had she kept her cell phone switched off?

On Wednesday, I noticed that Marie avoided looking at Lamadrid. It was as if they were trying to fool me, and didn't want me to see the intimacy between them.

Lamadrid had the gall to invite me to lunch. I took Marie, to see how far the two of them would go. It was pretty unpleasant. I ended up losing my composure when Lamadrid, whose mother was American, commented that the vigor of our orchestra had to do with our lack of tradition in classical music.

'Who told you that nonsense?' I asked. 'While your mother's ancestors were killing Indians, we were already composing motets for sixteen voices.'

'He didn't mean to offend you,' Marie commented later.

'And what's it to you? What's your interest in Mr. Forelock?'

At the end of the afternoon rehearsal, I canceled my appointments, and when Marie left the orchestra's garage I was already in my car, prepared to follow her. Itinerary: Consolação, Avenida Paulista, a different route from the one she usually took. She'd told me she was going home, but there we were, heading down Augusta. Marie didn't notice me even when she turned onto the peaceful streets of Jardim Europa. She parked in the garage at the home of her parents, who were traveling abroad. What better place for a tryst? Who would ever suspect?

I parked a block away and walked to the house, thinking that people are always just what we think they are. They're exactly that, nothing more. They never manage to be even a little better. But they can be terribly worse, that's for sure. There's no limit to how horrible and detestable they can be. How much they can lie and deceive. There's no end to that kind of crap.

I walked around the garden, circling the house; I went in through the kitchen and gestured to the maid not to announce me.

I found Marie in the living room, talking on the phone. She hung up as soon as she saw me.

'Hi, love. Are you all right?' she asked.

I ran a hand through my hair. I picked up the phone and hit redial.

'I came to see your father,' I said.

'WISP Security,' I heard a female voice say at the other end of the line. I hung up.

'My parents are away,' Marie said. 'I thought you knew. Who were you calling?'

I replaced the phone on the hook. 'The orchestra. It's busy.'

'I came to check out the burglar alarm,' she explained. 'It keeps going off; the repairmen will be here shortly.'

I stared at Marie. She began shuffling through the folders on the center table, which was covered with papers.

'Want to have lunch with me? Dalva is making some rissoles.'

I left after hearing the repairmen's opinion about the alarm, with a belly full of rissoles and feeling a bit idiotic, half-repentant, but that only lasted a few hours.

The next day, I woke up suspicious. I canceled some appointments just to be able to better follow the imbroglio. I checked Marie's cell phone, jotting down several numbers in 'calls received'. I called each of them, looking for clues. I verified the information she had given me. I phoned the dentist and asked if she'd been there. I did the same with the hair stylist, where she said she gotten her hair cut, despite the fact that I couldn't see a sign of any such cut.

I couldn't sleep that night. I waited for Marie to fall asleep and went to the living room, searching her wallet, appointment book, purse. I even checked the scores, her notes, looking for some secret code, some conspiracy. You'll find it, I told myself. Keep looking. Go through everything.

On the day of the concert, I felt especially bad. 'Do you think a man who's just been dumped for a scooter dealer can be that happy?' I asked Adriana.

'I've got to find out what antidepressants he's on. I want some for myself. Did you see how he combs his hair?'

I raced the orchestra so hard that night that I made Lamadrid look like a poisoned rat, skipping over phrases and desperately seeking me with his eyes. We had agreed upon a ritenuto for the final phrase, but I didn't stick to the suspended tempo, allowing Lamadrid to crash and burn on his own.

The concert was a disaster. But the audience, which someone once defined as 'that encompassing something that's nothing', probably didn't notice. The rabble never know anything. To them, everything is rice and beans, and what's good is to stuff yourself. The critics must have been happy too; after all, it's always more comfortable to destroy than to praise.

Marie came to my dressing room and asked what had happened.

'Ask the guy in the turtleneck,' I said, referring to Lamadrid. 'He was the one who ruined everything.'

I was quite agitated, and it bothered me to see how calm Marie was. 'Your calm burns a hole in my stomach,' I said. I also said that her way of looking at me, as if she understood me completely, put my nerves on edge. 'I hate your understanding. Why don't you scream sometimes? One of these days I'm going to teach you to kick doors.'

When Marie left the dressing room, with her air of superiority, my neck was so stiff that I could hardly breathe. There was no position in which I felt comfortable, and my back also ached badly. Maestros suffer constant back pain, believe me.

'You don't look good at all,' said Adriana, starting to massage the back of my neck. The touch of her hands was very nice. I felt warmth make its way down my spine. I stood up, quickly.

'I'm leaving,' I said.

Adriana tried to block my way. 'Don't you want me to give you a massage?' she asked.

I had already gotten in a lot of trouble because of that kind of thing and had learned my lesson well: when you want a massage, it's best to hire a Japanese.

17

ALL I HAVE TO DO is open my eyes and, bang, I'm wide awake, functioning. But that morning it was as if I had to be hoisted up from some far-off place, from a deep well, as if I were being towed to the surface, little by little. I heard footsteps around the house, muttered words, the incessantly ringing telephone, and from the bathroom came the pleasant aroma of shampoo. I couldn't move enough even to free myself from the blankets, even though I was sweating. That's the effect sleeping pills have on me, transforming me into a pâté of flesh without the strength to do anything. I opened my eyes, and even before asking Marie where she was going with those suitcases, I remembered a part of the dream I'd had during the night, in which I was taking off a man's head and later, terrified at being arrested, shoved the two parts of his body down a drain at the intersection of Iru and Bela Cintra. I told Marie. I said that, in the dream, someone had informed me that the drain I had used was the most sophisticated in São Paulo, as it had a highly efficient centrifuge system, and that I had chosen the best, taking into account the tragedy as a whole.

'Do you know whose head it was?' Marie asked, as she continued to fold clothes and put them in the suitcases. 'It's yours. You're tearing off your own head.'

I asked her if she was traveling, and she informed me with

great determination that she was leaving me. The turtleneck's revenge, I told myself, thinking that the only thing worse than being dumped for a scooter dealer was being dumped for someone who'd been dumped for a scooter dealer. I started laughing.

'Jânia told me everything,' Marie said.

I wanted to ask questions, or rather, to deny, to deny vehemently anything that Jânia might have made up, but it was as if I were blocked, stopped up. I remained in bed, paralyzed, observing the devastation. Marie made a long speech, saying that she couldn't understand how I could have been capable of paying our own maid to spy on her, that she had never thought I could do anything so petty, so sordid. 'Don't you have anything to say to me?'

I tried to say something, but the cavernous sound that came out of my mouth seemed more like a grunt.

'I suppose my phone is tapped too. Maybe you've hired some detective to follow me. Is that it? Just what did I do to make you act like this? How can you be so suspicious when you have a wife like me? I don't know if it's too much for you, but the truth is that I love you. Who was it that ruined you? It wasn't me. Or Teresa. Teresa, as far as I know, was a great wife. Then what's the matter? Why transform our life into this hell? Our kidding around about possessiveness is one thing, but what you're doing is something else. You're all the time saying you're not Jewish. That I can't forgive you for not being a Jew. Why the devil does that bother you so much? You're not a Jew. And nothing is going to make you a Jew. And I don't want you to be a Jew; if I wanted to be married to a Jew, I'd simply marry a Jew. You're even jealous of my reading about Israel. You go through my books to see what I underline. If I'm interested in who'll replace Arafat, if I'm interested in women in the Israeli army, if I read about the Muslims who volunteer as suicide bombers, if I'm glued to CNN, you're upset by it because it has nothing to do with you, it's not your issue. And you don't understand why you aren't the center of every last thing in my life. And if someone new comes to the orchestra the first thing that goes through your mind is that I'm going to throw myself into his arms. Know why I didn't go to bed with Rodrigo, with Sandorsky, with Lamadrid? Because I didn't want to fuck anyone. Nor they me. Maybe the only one who wanted that was you. Maybe the idea makes you happy. Maybe you need someone to betray you, the musicians, the orchestra, your employees, me. So you can say: Look, I was right, this is such a sonofabitch of a world that I have reason to hate. You have no friends. Who's your friend? So far, I've only seen you with the guest conductors. You don't even have room in your life for Eduarda. You hate everybody. You hate my mother. You hate my father. You hate Teresa. You hate my grandmother. You hate the concertmaster. You turn your back on the world, the world turns its back on you – I think that's how you've planned your life. I'm tired of that attitude. And of your foul moods. The horrible way you treat the musicians. In this house, the one who's doing the betraying is you. You betrayed me when you offered money to Jânia. I'll accept your apology. It won't keep me here, but it would be great if you could at least say you feel bad about all this. Say something. Please, say something.'

We remained silent for several minutes. Marie sat on the bed, hid her face, and sobbed for a time. It wasn't true that I'd paid our maid to spy on Marie. I just gave her money and grew tired of her expressions of gratitude. Her mother had an operation on her leg thanks to my money. Her nephew's computer class she also owed to me. Not to mention the TV and washing machine she had acquired. But people, as I've said, avenge themselves very well for the favors we do for them. Jânia had abused, had blackmailed me, and when I put an end to it by throwing her out, the she-devil rebelled and went to Marie with a pile of disgusting lies. I should never have offered her money. I don't even know why I did. I've never been religious, but there was inside me a force as powerful as the belief in saints or faith in God is for some, impelling me to take certain stances. For example, I made myself treat doctors well – despite the loathing I had for them – by 'believing' that if I wasn't nice to them I ran the risk of being told I had cancer. How could I explain that kind of idiosyncrasy to Marie?

I felt immense affection for her at that moment and wanted to sit at her side, dry her tears, explain the entire misunderstanding, but I simply did nothing. I let her cry until she got up and left, taking her suitcases.

As soon as Marie was gone, I turned on the television. It took some time for the broadcast to get to news about the Middle East conflict. Israel's antiterrorist policy would no longer be the same, said the report. Now Israel would reoccupy the Palestinian areas for as long as the acts of violence continued. In some way, those news items about Israel made me feel close to Marie. I thought about phoning her. But I felt unable to do anything.

I spent the rest of the morning in bed, beneath the comforter, with the air conditioning on, feeling hollow, without the courage to do anything at all. I didn't stir even when I heard Adriana's voice on the answering machine telling me that the president of the Symphonic Association was waiting for me at the orchestra.

I slept and woke several times, always with the sensation of having horrific nightmares, though I couldn't remember them. My head was throbbing, and when the bell rang I made it to the door only with great difficulty. If it's Rachel, I thought, I'll ask if she has any Fioricet. Actually, what made me get up was thinking that my neighbor would have more news about her daughter. 'She's having problems at the bank,' Rachel had said a few days earlier, 'because of another woman. You know, to destroy a woman there's nothing like another woman. I don't know how an orchestra works, but in real life that's how it is, you can never trust a woman. If you work with one, if she's above you in the hierarchy, she's going to squash you. And if you're a woman, worse still, because women not only want to take your place, they also want to destroy you.' Rachel had told me terrible stories about the battle Esther was facing, and since then I had asked her every day if her daughter had been fired. 'Not yet,' she would answer. Impressive how people put off making decisions. I don't know why that subject was so interesting to me, but sometimes during breaks in rehearsal I would call my neighbor to find out if anything had happened. There was an air of expectation, and I must say it had the effect of drawing me closer to Rachel.

When I opened the door, I saw Eduarda, my daughter, whom I hadn't spoken to for over three weeks. It was only when Teresa came out of the elevator with the dog and the suitcases that I remembered the promise I'd made three days before, on the phone. My ex-wife was going to spend the month away and wanted 'our daughter to stay with her father'. We had an argument about it at the time; I was deeply offended by the way she said 'stay with her father', accusing me of being an absentee parent. 'You *are* an absentee,' she said, 'that's not an accusation, it's a fact.' A shiver ran through my body when Teresa told me that, in addition to Eduarda, the dog would be staying with me. 'Cláudio and I can't take him.'

'Cláudio who?' I asked.

Teresa laughed. 'Don't play dumb.' Everybody knew about it, she assured me. It had even been mentioned on the society page, she commented with a certain degree of pride. She had always enjoyed reading the society page, that was the truth. When we were married, it was the first thing she would read. Even before checking to see if the paper carried a review of my concerts, before seeing the exchange rate for the dollar, all the tragedies, news of our disastrous economy, she looked to see who had gone to what parties, dinners, who had separated, and who had cheated. 'Those lowlifes,' she used to say, 'are a bunch of bumpkins, worms living off our flesh.' But now, apparently, the worms had turned and were good people. Teresa and Cláudio, my assistant, were linked in the society columns. 'Solid,' she emphasized. Cláudio was considering an offer to take over an orchestra in Fort Worth, Texas. They were leaving that night for the United States.

I didn't hear the rest of what Teresa went on to say; I went deaf for a few moments, dizzy, thinking that there was a time when I had liked Teresa so much, had so much affection for her, that I had even thought of killing her to spare her the sorrow of the divorce. When Marie returned from Israel and put our romance on an all-or-nothing basis, I spent days thinking about a good way of killing Teresa. I never wanted Teresa to suffer, never. And now she was telling me that she was going out with my assistant.

I had spent the last five years receiving accolades from Cláudio. There were times when the sonofabitch told everybody that I was his master; I should have suspected something, because no one lavishes so much praise without feelings of guilt. Even more so if you're a musician. Never believe that nonsense they tell you in dressing rooms. With us, praise is only given behind one's back.

I heard only the last part of Teresa's blah-blah-blah: 'We're involved.' That was the kind of expression that Cláudio loved: 'I'm very involved with Mahler,' he'd told me a few days earlier. My God, how could I not have seen it? All that talk about attracting an audience, which basically consisted of pleasing the mediocre, although he tried to glamorize the whole thing, by overvaluing the Ph.D. he'd done in Chicago, it was all part of the plan, and I hadn't seen any of it. He'd stolen my wife, and without a doubt he was taking away the orchestra too, the scoundrel. They were conspiring against me. Their dream was to remove me from the orchestra. And that's why he traveled so much, to disguise it. He said he was seeing orchestras outside the country, but deep down he really had his eye on mine.

'He's ten years younger than you,' I told Teresa.

'So what?'

'He's my assistant.'

'And so what?'

'Can't you see he's with you only because you're my wife?'

'I'm not your wife.'

The dog gave off a nauseating smell, so I went to get my camphor from the bathroom. When I returned, Teresa had left. I ran to the intercom: 'Ask Teresa to wait for me,' I told the doorman.

'If you want to talk about Cláudio, forget it,' she said when I got out of the elevator.

I didn't want to talk about Cláudio, I wanted her to take the dog with her, nothing else. I hesitated at bringing it up, experiencing a strange difficulty in articulating my ideas.

Actually, I was trying to decipher what was new about Teresa's face; I didn't immediately perceive that her lips were tumescent, prominent, that she had clearly injected some kind of crap into them. Why did women do that? Nowadays they all had those pouty movie-star lips. A sad way to grow old.

'You look very pretty,' I said.

She stared at me with disdain.

'Marie just left me,' I continued. I wasn't coming on to her, obviously. It never entered my mind that I might get back together with Teresa; I merely wanted to show her that my situation was complicated, I wanted to convince her to go back up to my apartment to take that enormous dog out of there. But Teresa misunderstood everything, thinking that I was suggesting a reconciliation. She started laughing and said, 'Don't be ridiculous. There's not the slightest chance for us, and you know why? Because there never was. I never loved you. It's only now that I realize that I was always unhappy with you. It took the separation for me to discover it. We have sex every day, Cláudio and I, you know what that's like? He worships me, he treats me like a goddess. And now you come to me with . . . Don't be ridiculous.'

'Go back there and get that dog!' I shouted, furious.

Teresa got into the car, still laughing and repeating, 'Don't be ridiculous,' then left. I stood there, remembering our separation. True, she had warned me. When I moved out, she had made a point of poisoning me with the words *husband*, *adultery*, *lover*, *lawyer*, and the phrase 'I'm going to destroy you.'

'I want you to be happy,' I had said at the time.

'And I want you and your happiness to fuck yourselves.'

In the elevator I thought that Teresa could only be seeking revenge by putting a Labrador in my apartment.

Seeing the dog completely at ease increased my irritation. I gave Eduarda money to get lunch somewhere. 'Take the dog,' I said.

I showered, got dressed, suffering. Not at Cláudio's betrayal; when you're a conductor you learn to deal with that, with perfidy. It's our first lesson: get away from those who call you master, because tomorrow they're the ones who'll pull the rug out from under you. I knew very well how to deal with that. What caused me so much agony was knowing that Marie had deserted me and there was a dog in my house. I called Homero before going out. 'Stop by,' he said, 'we'll talk.' So I did.

'How are things?' he asked, as soon as I settled into the armchair in front of his desk.

I recounted, frenetically, everything that had happened to me in the last few hours, the dog, the demonic violinist, Marie, Cláudio and his conspiracy. Homero listened to me calmly, then insisted on medication. I cut him off, spoke about my prodigious memory, the importance of conducting by heart, and how destructive chemicals were in that respect. I told him that after stopping the medication, besides being able to memorize the scores, I was able to put questions to myself like 'What was the first program I did in the 1986 season?' Or 'What did I have for lunch on Monday of last week?' I told him I managed to recall everything, or almost everything, although it gave me a lot of trouble. And a great sense of relief too, once the matter was solved. I would lay out complicated division problems for myself, without pencil or paper, and take a long time over them, but there would come a moment at which the numbers danced through my mind. None of that was good, according to Homero.

He spoke to me about my relationship with Marie, said

my jealousy wasn't normal, that everything I'd told him – about envy, possessiveness, suspicion, emulation, competition, rivalry, resentment, repetition, relief, fear of losing something – was illness provoked by a pathology. My disease had a name: obsessive-compulsive disorder, OCD, as the specialists say. 'That's why, for example, you phone Marie repeatedly; verification rituals are symptomatic of your disease.' He said that my bizarre behavior, my excessive and groundless suspicion of Marie, 'is all part of your disease'. Othello had such an illness. And José, in the opera *Carmen*. 'And Pozdnychev, remember? From *Kreutzer Sonata*? And to cite someone of flesh and blood, Freud. His wife's life was a living hell. Did you know that Frank Sinatra once interrupted a show to telephone Ava Gardner? Why? Because he was sick. A physical sickness, like cancer. We have scientific evidence which demonstrates that the sickness has to do with the reduction of serotonin in the body, an enzyme linked to self-esteem.' What I liked most was when Homero explained to me that the word *Eifersucht*, 'jealousy' in German, carries in its meaning the idea of playing with fire: *Eifer*, 'zeal', and *sucht*, 'mania'. In other words, jealousy is 'sick zeal'. 'You're sick,' he said, 'and you need treatment.' He said that my case would only get more complicated without medication.

The idea of going back on medication didn't appeal to me in the least. My arguments were more powerful than his; after all, what can matter more than our memory and a stiff prick?

I arrived at the orchestra feeling a little better. I spoke to the people in administration and told them to fire Cláudio. 'He's not under contract anymore,' they said. 'He refused to renew his contract.' That devastated me. Why hadn't they told me? Hadn't I ordered them to renew him? Yes, I had, but it was Cláudio himself who didn't want to. 'He's being paid on a per-concert basis,' they informed me.

I fired the orchestra manager. Maybe now they'd learn to obey my orders.

I worked all day, not thinking about anything, just working. Now and then an avalanche of memories swept over me. Marie, Cláudio and Teresa, the dog, and a bad taste would fill my mouth, acid. Every time that happened I called someone from my team, to hold a meeting.

That night, as I was leaving, Adriana asked me for a ride. She talked during the entire trip, but I was focused on her taut legs. When we got to the door of her building, she placed my hand on her knee and invited me to have a Diet Coke. 'Let's go up,' she said, 'it'll be good.' I was tired and sad. But I went up, and went to bed with Adriana.

18

'BREAKFAST IN BED,' said Adriana, coming into the bedroom completely nude, carrying two cans of Diet Coke, ice, and lime. I looked at the clock; it was past ten. She put the drinks on the night table, fluffed the pillows, and lay down beside me. 'Fucking's a good thing, isn't it?' After our fun and games, a confusion of sensations overcame me. Exhausted, dying to get out of there, I listened to the lengthy tale of Adriana's alcoholism, from when she began drinking wine with her father on Sundays to the episodes of vomiting, gutters, and scandal. What killed me more than anything was realizing that it made no sense, the two of us there. We could only lose, both of us. But Adriana, through some strange syllogism, had imagined that because I liked Diet Coke as much as she did, I could only be an ex-alcoholic myself, and therefore she considered me a 'special guy'. Quitting drinking, for some people, is a kind of religion. 'To tell the truth, I didn't like to drink. My thing was to get drunk. Don't you ever feel that way?' she asked several times. It did no good to explain that I'd never been an alcoholic; she went on treating me like one. At one point in our conversation I had the impression that I heard an I-love-you, which is why I got up so abruptly. I've never understood why women do that; as soon as they sleep with you they start talking of love, I thought, looking for my clothes. Putting sex and love in the same box must be a female pathology. We monkeys don't associate sex with anything. Sex is sex.

As I got dressed, I told Adriana I had read in the paper an item about the panda syndrome, a sexual shortcoming that occurs with those Asian bears. I explained that the animals, as large as gorillas, don't screw because it's so much work to stick the pinky-sized dick into the she-bear's pussy. 'The whole world's like that,' I said, 'nobody wants to fuck anymore. It's a lot of work,' I concluded.

Adriana went into the bathroom and came out in a satiny robe, with red roses. 'What's this panda talk?'

'Do you want to be a mother?' I asked.

'Is that part of the screening?'

'What?'

'I say "Yes, I want to be a mother", and you disappear.'

I hugged Adriana, laughing. 'The answer is no. No, I don't want to be a mother. I want to screw you. I want to be a lover, a girlfriend. I want you to fuck me and make me come. And I want to have fun. Does that make you feel any better?'

I said it did. 'You're fucked with me,' she said. 'Unlike the singers who show up at the orchestra, I'm intelligent. In fact, I used to think that stuff about singers being stupid was just talk, but today I know it's true. Those guys do nothing but listen, the world comes to them through their ears. They don't even read a cereal box. I even have a theory about the stupidity of tenors. The high pitch affects the brain. Creates a vacuum. I'm no singer. I have gray matter. Watch out for me.'

As I was getting into the elevator, Adriana grabbed me by the shirt and kissed me. 'And that I-love-you of mine was a lie. Don't believe anything I say when we're fucking, OK?'

It was infernally hot. I walked to the end of the block, covering my nose against the city's horrid smell and laughing at Adriana's attitude. 'Assistant,' as she liked to call herself. I wandered around a bit until I remembered that I had parked in the garage of her building. I went back; it wasn't easy to get into the garage, because I didn't understand the doorman, nor he me.

As soon as I got into the car, in that parking garage that smelled of disinfectant, I was overcome by a feeling of loneliness and isolation. I was paralyzed. I remembered Marie, just after we were married, nude, at my side, with a book that had a selection from the Code of Love, found in a twelfth-century manuscript. 'Listen to this. Rule Twenty-three: "He who is taken by thoughts of love eats and sleeps less." I eat and sleep less. Rule Twenty-five: "True love finds its good only in that which pleases the loved one." I only find my good in the things that relate to you, your music, your dick, your ideas. Rule Twenty-six: "Love can nothing love deny." I've never denied you anything, and I left Israel to live here. Rule Fifteen: "Every person who loves pales before the loved one." I've never gotten used to your presence, every time you appear in front of me the blood leaves my face. Rule Twenty-seven: "The lover can be sated only by the pleasure of his beloved." I'm only sated when you come. Rule Three: "A person who loves is occupied by the image of his beloved, tirelessly and without pause." And it's just that way, I think of you all the time, you, you, you.'

And now Marie had left me. I imagined her parents conspiring against me, in Hebrew. More and more they used that language in my presence, precisely so I wouldn't understand anything. I had mastered three languages, but they managed to make me feel inferior because I didn't speak Hebrew. I recalled a dinner at their house at which I asked, more from politeness than interest, about the conversion ritual for men. Monique had laughed at my question, which made me furious. Marie had later tried to placate me by insisting that it was startling for her parents, after having seen their own daughter claim her Jewish identity, to hear their non-Jewish son-in-law talk about converting. 'Really, they were moved. For a long time we lived as non-Jews; we didn't go to synagogue or belong to Israel associations. They were never concerned about passing on Judaism to me. But, as a teenager, I wanted to be Jewish. I went searching for my family's history, I wanted to go to Israel. It was because of me that they recovered the culture of community.' Marie made reference to the secularization of Judaism, 'Jewish indifference', but it did no good; of our entire conversation the only thing that rang in my ears was Monique's disdainful laughter. You don't speak our language, you don't belong. That was the significance of that raucous laughter.

I huddled over the steering wheel, my heart racing, a pressure in my chest. I was confused, I thought about going back to Adriana's apartment. Suddenly, I burst into laughter. It was always like that; I'd feel as if I had a bubble inside my chest, and when I tried to cry, either nothing would come out, or a guffaw like that, senseless.

Back at my apartment I found Eduarda watching TV. 'Dad,' she said. 'Not now,' I replied, heading for the bedroom. The dog followed me. 'Get away,' I said, 'leave,' but the dog lacked the least bit of intelligence. More than cats, fishes, more than any other animal, I hated dogs; the servility of the species set my blood on fire. I stomped my foot to scare it, and unintentionally stepped on its paw.

'Dad,' shouted Eduarda, coming to the aid of the dog, which was yelping exaggeratedly.

'I didn't mean to,' I said.

'His name is Nego.'

'What?'

'My dog is called Nego.'

'Take Nego out of here,' I ordered. Eduarda stared at me, perplexed. Only at that moment did I realize how much like her mother she was. Just like Teresa, the same accusatory gaze, the same critical bearing. The same tone of voice too.

I went back to the bedroom, furious at myself. Disoriented, experiencing every type of emotion, I called Marie's cell phone several times and left horrible messages. I called her an opportunist, said that she had only taken an interest in me in order to get a place in my orchestra, and that she was a rotten violinist.

I lay down, tried to read, but found no peace. I got up, paced around the room, distressed; it was as if something was forcing me to remain on my feet. I began searching the closets, not knowing exactly what I was looking for. There was nothing there. Empty drawers. Hangers without clothes. I counted the coat hangers. Then I leaned out the window and watched the movement below. Maybe Marie would come back. I counted nine dogs in five minutes. Marie wasn't coming back. Maybe that was a good thing. But that wasn't our game. She'd done her part, by leaving. The rest was up to me. The rescue was my responsibility. Suddenly everything was absolutely clear to me. The game was continuing after all. We were always going forward. I watched the passersby for a few more minutes; I liked the area. I showered, shaved, and went to Monique's house.

'She's not well,' my mother-in-law said, 'it'd be best if you talked some other time.' I ignored her and went into Marie's bedroom.

'Let's go home,' I said. 'Get your things.' Before Marie could answer, I opened her wardrobe, looking for a suitcase.

'Stop it,' she said. 'I'm not going back.'

'You have to call Homero. I've started treatment again.'

I opened the upper part of the closet. The bags were there.

'You frighten me. Just when I think you're all right –'

'OK, it was a mistake,' I said, cutting her off. 'Jânia never should have worked there. Where can I find a ladder?'

Marie sighed and gestured for me to stop what I was doing.

'It wasn't Jânia.'

I found an umbrella in the closet. I used the handle to try to reach one of the suitcases.

'Everything's all right,' I said. 'It's over. I've changed. I promise.'

Something in the closet was preventing the suitcase from coming out. I yanked on it. Nothing.

'Are you incapable of apologizing?'

'What's with this suitcase? I can't get it out.'

'Stop messing with my things. Drop that and apologize. It'll improve our situation.'

I yanked a bit harder, and suddenly the suitcase hit me on the head and fell to the floor, making a loud noise.

'I'm sorry,' I said. 'Sorry. You're absolutely right. I'm sorry.'

Marie picked up the suitcase. I sat on the bed, exhausted.

'Get your things,' I said.

At that moment Marie wasn't sure of anything; I could see she was confused, fearful. But despite that, she agreed to come home.

On the way back I felt neither happy nor sad. It would be different if she had just come back on her own.

19

'YOU LIE, YOU CHEAT, you're a lowlife, and you think everyone's the same way. That's your problem,' said Adriana.

We had just had sex, and here was Adriana, spoiling everything. 'Sure, I can be less unpleasant,' she said, 'all you have to do is turn off that cell phone and stop calling Marie every five minutes to find out where she is, if she arrived, if she left, and what she thinks about the chewing out you gave the musicians during the rehearsal. It's a bit much. I'm bothered by having to listen to those conversations, hear the two of you decide what film you're going to see tonight. And don't give me that I-didn't-promise-anything crap. This has nothing to do with relationships or with promises. Just with sensitivity.'

I left, irritated. I loved these trysts at Adriana's place in mid-afternoon, these moments of peace that she offered me, with a lunch we would make ourselves, everything was very good, but I was getting more and more impatient with that therapy-talk about my marriage. 'There's something neurotic about those incessant phone calls,' she would say. I admit I was overdoing it, but it wasn't a question of anything I could control. I only felt a degree of calm after hearing Marie's voice. If Eduarda answered the phone and told me Marie was in the bathroom, I didn't believe her. It was necessary to hear her voice. I feared that something bad had happened to her on her way to the orchestra. It was as if something bad were lurking all around us. The phone calls kept the danger at bay, that was the feeling I had. The more I phoned, the more everything was under control.

There were good moments between Marie and me. As soon as she returned, we took a few days off and went to New York. I was calm, slept all night, and felt up for things. We took long walks through the city, with no set destination, holding hands, going anywhere that interested us. Marie did some shopping, and I took the opportunity to see my American agent. We made plans for the future; it was great.

As soon as we arrived in São Paulo, I found a postcard from Lamadrid, addressed to me, saying that he was sorry about what had happened at the concert and that he hoped we could work together again in the future. 'P.S.: A hug for that adorable wife of yours.' I asked Marie what she thought of that 'adorable'.

'Nice.'

'You two became great friends, didn't you?'

'Professional contact.'

'But you showed him around the theater.'

'Out of politeness.'

'You told me it was because he asked.'

'Yes, he asked, and I was polite and showed him the theater.'

From that point, things only got worse for us. It was common for me to detain her in my room, after rehearsal, with questions of that nature. 'Tell me that story about Lamadrid again,' I would say. I would become possessed if I perceived any inconsistency in her answers, all of them jotted down in a notebook I'd bought especially for the purpose. I also liked to examine her purse, open her mail, and check receipts and phone bills. We fought a lot because of my attitude; she would lose patience, threaten to leave, I would backpedal, appeal, speak about my treatment, the daily twenty milligrams of fluoxetine I was forced to take because of her, which was a lie because I had never again set foot in Homero's office. In short, the game continued, with her winning and me feeling more and more unstable. To please her, I myself cut out the articles on Israel that appeared in the newspapers. Ten Palestinians killed. Five Israelis killed. Nineteen Palestinians killed. Ten Israelis killed. And so on. There was no end to bombs going off. But it wasn't just that. Israeli agents set up an ambush to kill a Hamas activist by hiding in a vegetable truck. And now the government of Israel was equipping foreign workers with gas masks. If the United States attacked Iraq, and Israel were to be attacked by Baghdad, they would be prepared. All this was in the newspaper clippings that I taped to our bedroom wall.

That night, I decided to change my method of checking on her.

'Say into this,' I asked her, showing her the recorder I'd bought, ' "There was nothing between Lamadrid and me".' I told her that this way we'd have an 'official statement'. I lied, saying it had been Homero's idea, 'to improve the quality of our relationship'. I was overly agitated, horrible thoughts kept coming into my mind, preventing me from concentrating on anything. I thought Marie would create a hell of a scene, but she simply took the recorder and made the statement, just as I had suggested.

The next day, we left at the same time for the rehearsal, in separate cars. Marie looked lovely, in jeans, her hair pulled back. 'I love you in jeans,' I said.

Before the rehearsal, I received word that she wasn't

coming; she'd felt ill on the way and gone to her parents' house.

Upon my return from lunch at Adriana's, I found Henri, Marie's father, in my room.

'The situation can't go on,' he said. I thought our conversation was going to be about financial markets or something of the sort.

'We found out that you aren't getting treatment. We spoke to Homero. We don't want Marie to go back to you. She'll stay with us from now on. That's final.'

After he left, I paced the room like a caged animal. I didn't want things to go their way. They needed to go my way. I called Homero and left a rude message with his secretary.

At six o'clock I called Henri and said I totally understood the situation but didn't want Marie to leave the orchestra. 'She's very talented. It would be a great loss for the orchestra and also for Marie. There's no other place she can play.'

'I'll speak to her,' my father-in-law replied. We ended on a friendly note.

That night, I tried to talk to Marie, but she refused to come to the phone. The next day, however, she showed up for rehearsal. Diffident, uncertain, she barely greeted me when she came onstage. Her mother remained in the audience the whole time, and smiled at me whenever our eyes met.

After the rehearsal, I called Marie to my room. She came, accompanied by her mother.

'Please, Monique, give us a moment alone,' I requested. She desperately wanted to be part of the conversation, but Marie persuaded her to wait outside with Adriana.

'It was the best solution for both of us,' Marie said once

we were alone. I let her talk a lot, taking enormous pleasure in hearing all those end-of-romance clichés that, at an earlier time, I had uttered to Teresa.

'I didn't want you to be mad at me,' was the final phrase.

'You're fired,' I said.

Marie stared at me, uncomprehending.

'You may go,' I ordered. 'Get out of my sight.'

'I thought –'

'You were wrong.'

Marie staggered out, before she began to cry, and Adriana came in immediately, with an air of satisfaction. She didn't even try to conceal having heard everything through the door.

'Maestro, you did the right thing. Best to nip it in the bud.'

I fired Adriana too. I'd had it with people thinking they understood me.

20

'Dearest Eduarda,

Cláudio has just been hired and is finally going to take over as artistic director of the Fort Worth Symphony. We're very happy, and today we rented a beautiful house with a large garden. You'll love it, sweetheart, the city is charming and just a few minutes from Dallas. Tomorrow I'm going to see about your school; I have an appointment with the principal. Hold on a bit longer, dear. Soon I'll be there to get you. Kisses from your adoring mother.

THE POSTCARD CAME WHILE Eduarda was at school. I was relieved to see that my daughter had an 'expiration date', as an old conductor friend used to say. 'That's the advantage of divorce. When the children come to visit, you know the day they'll be leaving.' I'd finally be free of that oversized dog whose specialty was sniffing women's crotches. That's all a Labrador does. But what really irritated me was the business about Cláudio and Fort Worth, that obvious climate of hostility toward me. 'Hold on a bit longer,' Teresa had written. What did that mean? That it was torture for Eduarda to live with her father? We'd been staying at the Caesar Park on Rua Augusta for two weeks, ever since I'd moved out of Marie's apartment.

As soon as Marie deserted me, Henri phoned to say he

would 'send someone' to pick up his daughter's things. 'No hurry,' he had said, 'you can stay in our apartment as long as you need to.' The rich love to feign indifference to material things. I told him I'd move out of their place that very day. I took absolutely nothing with me. Just some books of Marie's, because of the sentences she'd underlined. Nothing else.

If it weren't for my prestige, no hotel would have taken us with the dog. We stayed in two suites; Eduarda could only take the animal out through the service elevators, with the proviso of never crossing the lobby. Everyone went out of their way to make us feel comfortable there, but she always wore a critical or bored expression, clutching her small monster, listening to horrible music, or watching some piece of crap on television, never wanting to talk to me. But with her mother, on the phone, she was the picture of enthusiasm. She went into great detail, even describing what she was wearing, sometimes whispering and then exploding in guffaws that would send me totally out of control.

We had experienced happy, delicious moments like our trip to Rome; I had always been a loving father, and now she and her mother were treating Cláudio as if he were somebody. He'd never get anywhere, that guy. I was so anxious to say this to Eduarda that I didn't even leave the hotel before she returned from school.

'Hold on a bit longer, dear,' I read aloud, when Eduarda came into the bedroom.

'I don't mess with your things.'

'I suppose you have very pleasant things to tell your mother about living with your father.'

'All I said was that you don't like Nego.'

I yelled at Eduarda, told her she was just a kid and didn't know anything, not even that Cláudio was a traitor.

'You think everybody's against you,' she answered.

'Your mother left me for someone who for years has tried to take my place in the orchestra.'

'It was you who left my mother.'

I felt totally wild, and Eduarda's talking back like that maddened me. She had always been so obedient, and now she was defying me. Her and her mother, always on the same side.

'Go to Texas, go to Fort Worth. But you should know it's not Dallas,' I said. 'And don't come to me later saying you want to live with me.'

When we moved out of Marie's apartment I called Teresa to let her know we were staying at a hotel. 'How much longer are you going to make your daughter suffer because of the instability of your emotions?' Teresa suggested we go to her house: 'At least there Eduarda will find some comfort.'

The day had begun very badly. Nothing was right. The first days without Marie were unbearable. I would wake up, dab camphor around my nostrils so I could tolerate the smell of the hotel's carpet, then get the car and drive to the street where Henri and Monique's house was. I would stay there, as if in ambush, waiting for Marie to come out. At first I just wanted to see her. Later I began to follow her, noting the places where she had lunch or went shopping. And sometimes I tried to approach her. One Friday she was having ice cream on Oscar Freire and I got out of the car to return a book to her. She had underlined a sentence in it that I wanted to discuss: 'Everyone is worried about Israel [. . .] but do you know what worries me? Right here. The United States. Something terrible is happening right here. It feels like Poland in 1935. No, not anti-Semitism. That will occur in any case. No, it's crime, impunity, people who fear. Money – everything is for sale, and that's what counts. The young are filled with desperation. Drugs are merely desperation. No one has the desire to make himself feel so good unless he's profoundly desperate.' I wanted to tell Marie that I disagreed with that; the problem wasn't Israel or the United States. *Self-destruction* is the term that explains everything, I was going to say. We're all suicide bombers. We're living the moment of our own extinction. We're going to bring an end to everything. That's what I wanted to say.

But Marie didn't give me the chance to approach her. She refused to listen, tried to get away from me, and that's why we argued. 'Can't you see it's over?' she said on one occasion. 'What do I have to do for you to understand that?' Yes, I understood every word, but couldn't she come back to me? Couldn't she forgive me?

Later, things got even worse. I was no longer able to control myself around Marie. Our last encounter had been deplorable; after following her through the streets of Jardim Paulista and Jardim Europa, I pulled my car alongside hers at the traffic light, got out and started saying that she had never taken classes from Sandorsky, that the two of them were lovers and that I knew all about it.

Not even during rehearsals was I able to rid myself of the thoughts and horrible images that filled my mind. I remember going up to my room during the intermission in a concert and calling the academy in Tel Aviv, despite knowing from the time difference that it wasn't open. But, at the time, I imagined that Marie was taking advantage of the moments when I was conducting to telephone Sandorsky, and that they made contact through the academy, because the maestro was a married man. It was all so confusing. Why, for example, hadn't I considered the hypothesis of their speaking freely by cell phone? I don't know. The idea of the academy, the nocturnal phone calls, seemed a certainty.

I also can't explain why I again began thinking that Marie was having trysts with some of my musicians. I found no peace of mind, and I made an appointment with a private detective to ask about wiretaps. I even went to his office, on Consolação, and bothered him to no end. I said that, in my opinion, when a man thinks about tapping his wife's telephone he's already a certifiable cuckold. 'He's being betrayed for sure,' I declared. 'Not always,' the detective answered. 'We've had some pleasant surprises.' He refused to give me the numbers, but insinuated that he'd read somewhere that in ninety-nine percent of wiretaps there's proof of betrayal. 'We don't have stats,' he said, 'but anyway, what gets to you is the doubt, isn't it?' The guy knew everything about how to fuck with people's lives. He told me he was able to get into the files of any business, then offered me a choice of services. I said I'd think about it, and never went back. I felt disgusted by all of it, including myself.

At that time I was seeing Leontina, a Russian violoncellist who was a good friend of Marie's. Russians pronounce *o* and *u* as *ah*. They say *sahn of a bitch. Albaquerque*. I don't even know why I'm mentioning this, maybe because the appeal of my relationship with Leontina was merely that; I was all the time trying to teach her to pronounce *o* and *u* properly. But it was she who told me that Marie had been invited to audition for the Fort Worth orchestra, with Cláudio.

That happened the same day Eduarda received the postcard from her mother which made me sure there was a conspiracy against me. They were attacking me from all sides, simultaneously. We were having lunch together,

Leontina and I, and she seemed pleased with the news. She thought it would be good for a Brazilian musician to play in a foreign *archestra*, as if Fort Worth were a great orchestra and not merely some second-rate provincial orchestra. But that's how Russians are; to them anywhere is wonderful, even Texas.

After lunch, I called Hannah, my agent, and asked how to contact the people in Fort Worth. 'What do you want with them? Can I be of any help?'

No one could help me. I got the numbers and immediately phoned the orchestra. An Alberta answered and informed me that the manager hadn't yet arrived. That's all I let her say. 'You've just hired Cláudio as conductor, a lowlife who'll destroy anything musical there,' I said. I told her how I had fired him, and that I'd also fired Marie, the young woman who was going there to audition as violinist. The woman tried several times to interrupt me – Americans can't stand one being anything but pathologically direct; if you offer any kind of preamble they get desperate because they think they're wasting time. Nothing is more exasperating for an American than the sensation of wasting time. To them, it's very primitive to waste time, even to residents of Fort Worth. I didn't let Alberta interrupt me.

'I can't allow unqualified professionals to use the name of my orchestra to obtain positions in yours.'

'There's no one from administration here at the moment. Call back later.'

I left my name and number, requesting that the orchestra manager contact me. 'It's urgent,' I said. I hung up, dying to chew out someone. Sometimes that was how I calmed down, by bellowing at others. That day, however, the people in the orchestra were doing things right. Rosa, the new secretary, was very efficient. She had been unemployed for eight months and, like everyone who came to work for us, had developed an interest in music. The first time we were alone, she told me she was 'crazy about Liszt. Do you like Liszt?' I didn't tell her that Liszt was what could be considered the 'middle class of composers'; maybe one day she would realize it on her own. 'Listen to the piano pieces,' I replied. 'What about Wagner?' she asked. *Tannhäuser* is crap. *Lohengrin* is quasi-crap. The only Wagner that's worth anything is *Tristan und Isolde* and the *Ring*. I didn't say any of that, let her fuck herself.

'Shall we take a look at the schedule?'

To tell the truth, I missed Adriana. I had called her several times, leaving messages, but she didn't call back.

That afternoon, I decided to go by her place. Adriana opened the door, and even before I perceived her state of intoxication I smelled the strong odor of vodka.

Only one slipper, dirty nightgown, her hair in disarray – I felt sorry for Adriana. She hugged me tightly, muttering things like 'Let's fuck', 'I'm dying to have somebody go down on me'. I carried her to the bedroom.

I placed her on the bed, went to the kitchen, thinking about heating up some milk, but there was nothing in the refrigerator. I needed a fresh application of camphor around my nose to move about in that mess, empty bottles, the remains of food in pots that must have been there for days.

When I returned to the bedroom, Adriana was asleep. I phoned the orchestra and told Rosa to arrange for a cleaning lady, emphasizing that it was a private matter and I would pay for it personally. I called Mário, Eduarda's driver, and gave him a list of purchases, asking him to deliver them to Adriana's house.

Marlene, the cleaning lady, arrived by four o'clock. She tidied up the place, washed the clothes, the kitchen, the bathroom, helped put away the things that Mário had brought me, and then prepared some chicken soup.

Adriana didn't wake up until eight, still a bit drunk. I helped her into the shower, bathed her, put clean clothes on her, and combed her hair. Then I made her eat the soup, placing spoonfuls in her mouth. I changed the sheets on the bed, and she went back to sleep.

I called the hotel. Eduarda had gone to walk the dog, they told me at the front desk. I leafed through several magazines, with the TV tuned to an interview program in which a politician was saying that Israel should 'buy territory in another region'. I phoned Marie at her parents' house, but by now the maids automatically said she wasn't in. 'Tell her to turn on Channel Thirteen,' I said. I wanted Marie to hear the absurdities the interviewee was uttering. 'But why does Israel have to leave there and not the Palestinians?' asked the journalist. 'The Palestinians occupy a greater area and are more numerous.'

I went on listening to the guy's idiocy for a few more minutes, then fell asleep on the sofa. At midnight I awoke to Adriana's voice. She wanted to know what I was doing there. She didn't remember a thing – the shower, the soup, 'I'll bet it wasn't you who cleaned up.' I showed her the provisions, said I thought she was very thin, that she had to take care of herself. I asked if she needed money and offered to help her. With an unhappy look on her face, Adriana asked me to leave.

'You need to get help.'

'Does it make you feel good?' she asked.

'What?'

'This farce of helping me.'

'If you're asking if I feel guilty because you've started drinking again, no. No, I don't.'

Adriana got up, she was so fragile that I felt pity for her. She lit a cigarette. 'I'm smoking too now,' she said. Then she opened the door, called me 'scum-sucking maestro', said she neither needed my 'idiotic advice' nor wanted to hear it. And that, yes, I should feel guilty about her drinking again. 'I love you,' she said.

We stood there in silence for several moments, my gaze fixed on the floor.

'I wanted you to come back to the orchestra,' I said.

'Why?'

'You were the best secretary I've ever had.'

'Fuck you.'

Adriana waited until I left. Inside the elevator I could still hear her sobs.

I didn't stop by Eduarda's suite to see if she was all right and say goodnight. I tried to reach Marie on her cell phone, but she had changed her number.

I thought about going there, entering the house, but for a moment it all seemed senseless. What would I say to Marie?

I took a sleeping pill.

21

THERE WAS NO REHEARSAL that morning. I sat in the audience area, in a darkened hall, with my eyes closed, listening to the silence. I don't know who said that life without music is simply a mistake, but it's as true as saying that life without silence is a mistake. That was one of the reasons I felt so good in the seats at my concert hall. There I could find peace. With all the doors closed, I would sink into one of the chairs, totally cut off from the outside world, hearing the sound of silence, which no longer exists anywhere else.

As soon as I entered my room, Rosa came with the news: 'We have a request from the federal government, they want to make use of our space for a samba-school show as the closing event of the international debate on sustainable development,' she said, enthused. I told her to call them and say that unfortunately it would be impossible. 'The purpose of this space is symphonic,' I explained.

'But it's the president,' she insisted.

'Samba schools don't come through those doors. They degrade the acoustic quality of the hall.'

'Our marketing director said it's not a bad idea to use our space for popular events.'

'The event isn't popular. It's for rich businessmen to ogle the asses of mulatto women. The day we get invited to play at a samba site, I'll give the matter some thought.'

That morning, I had woken up restless; the sleeping pills weren't providing me with peaceful nights anymore. I woke up late, took a quick shower, and checked Eduarda's suite before leaving. The maids had already made up her bedroom, and the dog wasn't there. I couldn't imagine what she'd done with the animal, and it didn't occur to me to ask the hotel staff.

I spent the rest of the morning at the orchestra, talking on the phone. The administrator in Forth Worth called me back, but by then I'd lost the desire to continue the campaign against Cláudio. 'Cláudio is an excellent musician,' I told her, sincerely. I ended up inviting them to play for us. Next I called Hannah in Switzerland, and must have seemed very confused.

'So what is it you want, after all? Did you or didn't you invite Fort Worth to play in Brazil?' she asked.

I explained that all she had to do was ignore them, and not follow up on anything.

'Follow up on what? I wasn't the one who spoke with them. I didn't extend the invitation. It was you who started this whole business. I don't understand this conversation. Are you all right?'

The consequence of the confusion I'd created vis-à-vis Fort Worth was obvious. With the expectation of playing in Brazil, the directors of the orchestra would end up approving Marie after her audition. The administrator must surely have assumed that I was still Marie's husband, and must have concluded that I'd made the invitation because of that. An exchange. She OKed Marie, and I invited the orchestra to play in Brazil. I was going to explain all that to Hannah, but it was just too much trouble. She wasn't in a good mood. As soon as she answered the phone she started complaining, badmouthing her artists. I calmed her by also speaking badly of everyone, then got off the line at the first opportunity. I continued to ruminate about my problem and came to the decision that they wouldn't take Marie away to live in Texas. It was just a matter of time before she came back to live with me. It wouldn't be Fort Worth that would ruin everything.

Thinking this way, I parked facing the house of Marie's parents, and prepared to wait for her. I was in the car, waiting, when I saw a man placing a sign – 'for rent' – on the lawn of the house on the opposite side of the street. I was attracted by the idea of living in that location. From there I could keep constant watch on Marie, monitor her every movement with relative ease. I called the real estate agency, put them in contact with my secretary, and minutes later received a call from the owner: 'I'm friends with your father-in-law,' he said. 'I'll rent to you with the greatest pleasure, maestro. By the way, let me compliment you on the presentation of *Rake's Progress*. I went prepared. I read Auden's libretto. How wonderful!' Lately I enjoyed great popularity here. Someone was always coming up to me and saying he'd liked the concert, the programs, which was very gratifying.

As I was listening to the owner's praise, the garage to Marie's parents' home opened and her car pulled out onto the street. I ran and stood in front of the automobile.

I asked her to roll down the window, but Marie acted as if I were a carjacker. I felt like smashing the window. The security man left his post and approached. I banged on the glass. 'Open this piece of crap,' I said.

Marie rolled down the window, but not all the way. She was afraid of me.

'Did you get my message?' I asked.

'Say what you have to say, I'm late.'

'Why don't you answer my calls?'

'You're a real barrel of problems. And I've about had it. Why don't you see a doctor? Your case is medical. I'm sorry, but I can't help you.'

'I know about your plans with the Fort Worth orchestra.'

Marie didn't react.

'Without a letter of recommendation from me, you'll never be accepted,' I said.

'We'll see.'

'"What damned minutes tells he o'er/Who dotes, yet doubts, suspects, yet strongly loves!"' I recited.

Nothing. She was unshakable, Marie.

'You've never read Shakespeare, have you?' I said.

Another nothing in reply. It occurred to me then that Cláudio might very well be interested in Marie. That explained the invitation.

'Does Cláudio want something from you?' I asked.

'You think I don't have any musical talent? Is that your judgment? I want to work,' she said. 'And Cláudio is offering me the opportunity. That's all.'

I started laughing. 'Is that the latest thing with the rich? In the old days the rich wanted to have nothing to do with work.' I felt like saying that she was totally and exclusively mine and that she had no right to play for Cláudio, or for any other orchestra, but for some reason I managed to contain my aggression. I mean, more or less.

'You're not going to pass the audition,' I said. 'Not this one or any other. I know all the agents. Nobody wants to hire you.'

Marie gunned the motor and left me standing there, alone.

As I was returning to the orchestra, ready to phone every agent in the world and ask them not to hire Marie, my phone rang. It was Mário, the driver. He asked what was going on with Eduarda. She wasn't in the hotel that morning when he'd come to take her to school. He had called her room and when she didn't answer had assumed she'd spent the night at a girlfriend's, as had happened several times. But now he'd gone to get her at school and discovered that Eduarda had missed class.

I went straight to the hotel. Maybe Teresa knew something.

'You're worrying me,' she said on the phone. 'We spoke yesterday, she called and said she was going to take Nego for his walk and then study for a math test.'

Eduarda didn't answer her phone. Leontina went to the hotel, as did Rosa. We began calling all her friends, every acquaintance, a lot of work because I knew absolutely nothing about my daughter's life, not even what grade she was in at school. The principal became rather indignant when she realized how ignorant I was.

The hotel manager, apprised of the situation, spoke to me. Employees on the night shift had seen Eduarda leave with the dog, but they hadn't seen her come back.

That worried me. In my daughter's room I found her handbag with all her documents; nothing indicated that she had planned to spend the night elsewhere. The maids said that in the morning the bed was made, as if no one had slept in it.

Teresa began calling every five minutes. 'You're telling me you don't even know whether she slept in the hotel, is that right? What the hell kind of father are you?'

In the middle of all those phone calls, the owner of the house across the street from Marie's parents called to say he'd changed his mind and no longer wanted to rent it. Obviously, he had spoken to Henri. But at that moment the house was the thing that mattered least.

By the end of the afternoon, with no word of Eduarda, I was so tense I couldn't even sit down.

'I think we should start checking the hospitals,' the hotel manager said. 'The morning porter said that yesterday someone was run over on Avenida Paulista.'

It was midnight when Leontina called me from the morgue. The accident victim, a teenage girl, had been taken there with no ID.

'It's not Eduarda,' I said.

'She had a dog with her,' Leontina replied. 'I think you should come here right now.'

I don't really know how I got to that place, everything I remember is very confused, people were talking to me but I couldn't hear them. The smell was horrible, and I felt nauseous. We went into a totally gray room. A young worker uncovered the body that lay on the metal table.

It was Eduarda.

22

I WOKE UP WITH the television tuned to First Combat. 'You missed the match between Ronnie Lynn and Mark Smith,' said Leontina, who since Eduarda's death had come to live with me at the hotel. 'You also missed Steve Malcon and Brad Dickson, but it wasn't anything great. It ended in the fifth round with Dickson looking like a blood sausage.' I was impressed by her recent knowledge of wrestling; she liked to note down the rankings of our favorite wrestlers – Leon Bruce, Warwick, Burn – although afterward she never knew where she'd written the results. 'When you're Russian you're very much interested in that business of hitting and getting hit.'

I had spent the weekend doped up on the sofa, in front of the television. Sometimes I managed to get up and eat some crap or other, go to the window, but all of it demanded great effort.

On Saturdays, after the final concert of the week, I would begin what I called 'Homero's Molotov' – Xanax, Lexotan, Versed. My psychiatrist had prescribed a series of medications; I took several of them and felt perhaps not all that different from the people who'd gone to my daughter's wake, those people who are simply in our life by chance, randomly, by coincidence, those acquaintances, ex-friends, ex-musicians, former neighbors, wives of people you don't even remember anymore, distant uncles, distant cousins, those people who don't care about you but make a point of coming to your daughter's wake and suffering the proper amount, and a still bigger point of forgetting it all the minute they go home.

Psychotropic drugs, in one sense, do that to us; with them we suffer in the way that those who have nothing to do with our story suffer. Like those who read about it in the paper. Like the people who kept looking at me at the wake, as if they understood perfectly the tragedy of a father whose only daughter, fourteen years old, is run down by a bus on Avenida Paulista. Those were my thoughts as I heard the expressions of condolence during the wake. Even maestro Elias showed up. I thought he had died, and then the old lion appears, decrepit, eager to console me. He looked at me as if, in the matter of losses, he were superior to me. I remembered the last time I'd seen him conduct, that unruly head of hair on the stage, the strings meowing, the brass shrieking, I left in mid-concert. And there he was at the wake, contemplating my pain.

'If they'd had Rivotril in the Middle Ages,' Rachel, who was also an expert in pills, told me, 'God wouldn't be so popular.'

At the wake, a girl approached, leading by the hand a young man who couldn't be more than sixteen. Tall, good-looking, with bloodshot eyes that wouldn't meet my own.

'Maestro, this is Eduarda's boyfriend.'

For the rest of the time, I stayed at the side of Eduarda's boyfriend, and his silent presence, I can't explain why, was the only thing that brought me any kind of comfort.

During the week, the routine of the orchestra kept me busy full-time. Anything that wasn't music was put aside. That was what I could call peace in those days. Only in that way was I able not to think about Eduarda, about her slight body stretched out on the metal table in the morgue. As soon as I recognized my daughter, a worker from the coroner's office handed me an envelope with her personal effects: mint-flavored chewing gum, and a blue hair clip with childish markings.

They say that Toscanini conducted the night after the death of his four-year-old son. After that night in the morgue, Toscanini came to be my example. I've never worked as hard as in that period. There were days when I felt so agitated that after rehearsals, not having anything more to do in my room, I would go through the bathrooms to check the toilet paper. I even helped a custodian scrub out a stain on the floor of the lobby. 'Don't do that,' Rosa said when she caught me there. 'You're the conductor. Please, it doesn't look good.'

My rehearsals were a kind of battle with the musicians. At one, a third-chair violin laughed and I yanked the bow out of his hands and threw it into the seats. It didn't make me happy to see the ill feeling engendered by my shouts and curses. They were afraid to breathe for fear it would displease me. I wasn't, as usual, merely demanding that they be superb. I wasn't being merely rigorous. It was not just music that I was making there. It was also an exercise in survival, a way of keeping my underground from surfacing.

Good thing, I thought, that I have my orchestra in Brazil. I might have committed suicide over Eduarda's death if I were the conductor of the New York Philharmonic. I'd blow my brains out if my adviser were one of those American professionals who hit the streets and return to the orchestra with a bagful of money. Nothing around me worked the way I wanted it to. It was necessary to scream, curse, fire people, offend, threaten, and that took up all my time. There is no internal hell that can flourish under such circumstances. True pain needs a less demanding atmosphere. You can't suffer to the full with so much to be done. Thus I held myself together during the week. But after the Saturday concert I would crumble. 'You should talk to your doctor about Rivotril,' Rachel insisted, believing her medication was better than mine. 'Did you know that Rivotril is for epileptics? When I read that in the insert I was shocked. Why did my doctor prescribe it for me? I'm just depressed. I'm desperate. I have a daughter who's been running around with the minister of finance and who was let go from the bank where she worked. And who until a short time ago hated me and now needs me. And who's pregnant by somebody or other. Did you know that, maestro, that Esther is pregnant? Almost forty, and pregnant. I don't have a clue who the father is. All she does is cry, all day long. The other day, the doorbell rang, and when I opened the door she threw herself into my arms, crying like an eight-year-old. And calling me mother. You know, that strong executive who always wore suits and gave her mother nothing but grief? That woman doesn't exist anymore. That woman is a hollow shell. And so am I. Both of us are wrecks. The difference is that with Rivotril I still function. When I read the insert and saw that it was medicine for epileptics, I thought: after all, what am I? What's the difference between me and an epileptic? That's just what I am. Epileptic. The word totally describes me. I'm neurotic, old and epileptic. You're epileptic too. You ought to ask Dr. Empédocles for Rivotril.' Rachel still hadn't learned the name of my doctor.

That Monday, I had breakfast in my bedroom. Leontina was looking after me with affection, choosing the clothes I wore, serving and sweetening my milk, spreading jelly on my toast. I was grateful to her for that. 'Get me my glasses, sweetheart. My pills. My coffee. My this. My that. You're always asking for things, every time I walk by you assign me some task,' Marie once said to me. 'You have the habit of thinking that everybody has to wait on you. You're like my father. My father is always surrounded by secretaries, so when he gets home he goes on giving orders, as if he were at the office.' Marie would never take on that role, unlike Teresa, whose 'servitude to her husband', as she herself put it, had been her main activity for many years. 'My entire youth,' she never tired of saying. 'I gave up my career because of you.' No one remembered anymore that Teresa had once studied violin; even she had admitted thousands of times her lack of musical talent, but that phrase had been a kind of slogan that she had used for the greater part of our relationship, to the point where one day I thought, after an attack of amusement, that I could introduce her to new friends by saying: this is Teresa, who gave up the violin to be with me.

I showered and went to meet Teresa. She and Cláudio would be returning to the United States that night, and I had agreed to go by her house, I don't really know what for, perhaps to give her one last opportunity to tell me how she held me responsible for our daughter's death.

When Teresa arrived back in Brazil, we'd had a moment of affection. 'Why?' she asked, weeping. But later, when we met at the crematorium, Teresa blamed me for Eduarda's death, saying I was selfish and that I didn't know what was going on with our daughter, that on the night on the accident I hadn't even noticed that she had not slept in the hotel, that it all could have been avoided if I had been more aware. 'A shitty father,' she said. 'A huge piece of crap, that's what you've always been.'

It was past eleven when I got to Teresa's. I waited in the living room, while the workers wrapped packages and covered the furniture. I could already smell the odor of an abandoned house. For years and years, in my youth, I had lived in that type of residence, whose occupant is never present. I was always traveling and would stay at friends' houses; they in turn were also out in the world, conducting at concerts. Teresa's house had already been transformed into such a place, devoid of spirit, where however alone you may be, you find no peace.

The urn containing Eduarda's ashes was on a table beside the fireplace. It came to me that I would like to offer an homage to my daughter, that I could scatter a handful of that matter, which had once been hers, into the sea, or in a garden; there was an indisputable energy there, and maybe that, that cycle, was what we call immortality. I felt great relief in thinking this. At least there was that. Matter. I picked up a small metal box that Teresa had used as a table decoration, and as I was opening the urn Teresa burst into the room, followed by Cláudio. She practically attacked me when she saw the urn in my hands. She grabbed it away from me, furious. 'You're not keeping anything.'

I explained my intention. 'I don't want it all,' I said, 'just a handful.' I mentioned the homage.

'A handful? Is that what you just said? A *handful* of your daughter?'

Before going upstairs, Teresa slapped me in the face.

Cláudio and I stood there in silence for a time.

'Take care of Teresa,' I said, to close the subject. He walked me to the garage. I was already getting into the car when I decided to ask a favor. The atmosphere was in no way favorable, but I didn't even hesitate.

'Don't take Marie to Fort Worth,' I asked. That was the last time I saw them.

Now Marie: I had seen her at the ceremony of farewell to Eduarda. We didn't exchange a single word, merely standing arm in arm at the moment of cremation. She was trying to comfort me, and I felt no relief at all. Just the opposite: her presence made me more agitated and depressed.

Some days later, I phoned her house and asked her to come to the hotel. It was a Thursday, and Leontina was playing in the orchestra under the baton of a guest conductor.

At nine o'clock, Marie called me from the hotel lobby and suggested we have something in the restaurant. I insisted she come up.

'I thought I would run into Leontina,' she said as she entered my suite.

I made a formal invitation, said I would like very much for her to return to the orchestra, and that we could put all the nonsense behind us.

'You're a great violinist. My orchestra needs you.'

'I don't want to.'

'Why?'

'I just don't want to anymore, that's all.'

'But you did before.'

'I know. But I don't want to play there anymore. Not because of you. Because of us, I mean. It won't work anymore.'

I remained silent for several minutes. Marie got up.

'He doesn't want you to play there anymore?' I asked.

'My father?'

'No. The guy you're seeing.'

'You fired me, didn't you? There isn't anyone.'

'I fire and hire whoever I want. The orchestra is mine. Mine. Tell him that.'

'Who are you talking about?'

'You're seeing someone. Who is it?'

'You should try to be happy with Leontina. She's a great girl.'

'Who is he? I want to know.'

Marie went to the window. 'Did you ever trust me? At any time? Didn't it ever go through your mind that I was faithful to you? That I truly loved you?'

'Rodrigo?'

Marie sighed, upset.

'No,' I continued. 'I'll bet it was one of the horns. A heroic instrument with a broad repertoire. You like horns, horns are God. If you don't screw the maestro, it's best to screw the horns. I don't think you screwed the oboes. They're too neurotic. You don't have the patience to wait for them to trim those reeds all day long.'

Marie picked up her purse.

'None of that. Stay here. I'm trying to guess. I can guarantee you had nothing to do with the flutes. They're snobbish, Frenchified, and you've had enough of that, haven't you? Monique exhausted your quota of upturned noses. Or with the violas, you don't like those violinists manqués. Or with the trombones, the farters of the orchestra, the whore-hoppers, the ones who watch video porn – you find all that very vulgar. Or with the clarinets, those timid types, you like the powerful ones, don't you? Let me see . . . Of course, the brass, who are potheads like you. Or the tympanis, who are just as wild. The strings? Don't tell me you screwed the strings. The strings are the most uninteresting people in the world. The only ones worse than the strings are ballet dancers, who think about nothing but their feet. I know. You screwed all our cellists. That beautiful, sensual instrument, those men hugging the instrument. It's very pretty. Tell me, I'm curious. Musicians are yokels who only think about playing the perfect note, and every bit as imbecilic as dentists, who only think about prostheses. Tell me. Was it Haroldo?'

'I'm leaving Brazil,' she said.

'No, don't go,' I replied. 'Who is he?'

Neither of us spoke.

Marie was about to say something, then changed her mind. She headed for the door; I did the same, placing myself in her path. I don't know why she became so desperate, or why she started screaming that way. I just wanted to talk, just wanted her to tell me the guy's name.

'Get out of my way!' she shouted.

And then Leontina opened the door and came in. It was all very fast and very awkward.

Marie left, and we haven't spoken since.

It was a horrible night. I felt an enormous need to tell her there wouldn't be any audition in Fort Worth. I called her parents' house several times; the servants hung up the phone when they heard my voice.

'A sensational match with Roy Sanders is about to begin,' Leontina told me when she saw me on the telephone cursing the pantryman at Marie's house.

I didn't answer. I kept dialing incessantly.

'She doesn't want to talk to you,' Leontina insisted.

'Would you do me a favor?' I asked. 'Call her house. Say you're a friend.'

'No. That's ridiculous. In Russia there's a name for it: humiliation.'

'All you have to do is get her on the line.'

'How can you love a woman who –'

I didn't let her finish. 'I'm asking you for a favor,' I said.

Leontina was slow to act. She stared at me in a way that was simultaneously critical and distant. She picked up the phone, dialed Marie, and handed me the telephone.

'You're not going to run away anywhere,' I bellowed when I heard Marie's voice at the other end of the line. 'Cláudio doesn't want you in Fort Worth. He told me so himself.'

Silence.

'You're finished as a musician, Marie. No one will have anything to do with you.'

Marie hung up the phone, not wanting to hear the other things I had to say – although I couldn't remember what they were. I sat down for a few moments, organizing my thoughts before a new assault. I would destroy her. I thought about asking Leontina to call again. But by then my Russian woman was packing her bags. She had decided to leave.

In any case, it wouldn't do any good to ask Leontina to intercede. There was nothing in the world that would get Marie back on the phone that night.

23

THE ABRUPT VARIATIONS OF Camargo Guarnieri are like an old Volkswagen microbus with a busted exhaust. You never know when you're going to hear a blast, and suddenly, pow, the driver in the next lane gets a terrific scare. After you familiarize yourself, those violent breaks in rhythm and the uneven pulsation of Guarnieri's symphonies no longer impress you, and you come to see the composer as he is: round, predictable, unsophisticated. The true genius was Villa-Lobos. I can't help thinking, as I rehearse, that Guarnieri must have hated him, even though he said he greatly admired him. Villa-Lobos must have made him generate enough bile to poison a battalion. Who said that every contemporary is detestable? And that it's easy to admire the dead genius, but we never resign ourselves to the live genius breathing beside us, eclipsing our talent? I imagine that Camargo Guarnieri truly desired the death of Villa-Lobos. Being his contemporary was a kind of punishment for him. God gave him the gift, and the devil gave him Villa-Lobos. I imagine that his *Uirapuru* was not an homage to Villa-Lobos. It was an attempt to forgive his rival.

These were my thoughts during the rehearsal. I simply couldn't give myself over to the music; my head was flying free, out of control.

'Excuse me, ladies and gentlemen, I made a mistake.' I

erred several times, and there was one moment when I felt it necessary to check the score of Guarnieri's *Sinfonia número 2*, which I knew by heart. I asked for it to be brought to me. While my assistant went to get it, I left the stage and called Marie's old cell phone eight times. I knew she had changed numbers, knew that the phone was deactivated, but I felt compelled to do it, and I can even say that calling that number, which belonged to no one, so many times, hearing that metallic voice of the recording – 'The number you have called is not in service' – had a certain calming effect on me.

The score arrived, and I resumed the rehearsal, tumultuously. I was irritated by the way the musicians looked at me. It wasn't like it used to be, with them awaiting my commands, they were no longer instruments that I played. Ever since Eduarda's death they had looked at me differently. It was as if they had suddenly come to like me. Now they admired me, not because I was the conductor, but because I was a man of misfortune suffering over the death of his teenage daughter, and that had made me their equal. At the cremation, I had noticed that it wasn't solidarity they were showing but a sick curiosity, as if they wanted to ask: So, maestro, how goes your suffering? How does the pain inside work? The fuckers felt sorry for me.

The rehearsal continued to be a catastrophe. I called one of the flutists an imbecile and drove the musicians to exhaustion by repeating several sections. I yelled at my assistant for informing me that it was noon. 'This isn't a factory,' I replied, although I myself demanded that rehearsal times be rigorously observed.

For the rest of the day I felt awful. I saw a group of adolescents walking along Augusta, noisy, giggling girls who had just gotten out of school, and it tore my heart apart. Usually I slept for an hour before a concert to achieve greater concentration. That evening, however, it was as if something was poisoning me. I couldn't lie down, or sit, or walk the streets; everything made me uncomfortable, anguished.

I got into the car and went to Marie's parents' house, determined to resolve the situation. I said as much at the wheel: 'I'm going to solve this business once and for all,' despite having no idea how to do it.

I parked the car and waited. I watched the servants take the dogs out to shit in the streets. It was almost an hour before Marie appeared, nosing her car into the garage. When the electronic gate opened, I went in with her.

Marie grimaced with annoyance when she saw me and didn't even say hello as she got out of the car. She turned her back on me, and I followed her into the house, disconcerting the domestic staff with my presence.

'Don't make me be rude to you,' she said when we got to the living room.

'Be rude,' I answered. 'Please, be rude.'

I sat down on the sofa.

'I'm afraid of you,' she said. 'Every time you come near me I'm terrified.'

'Continue.'

I listened as Marie said she didn't know what to do anymore, that our marriage had been a 'veritable hell', a string of interrogations and investigations. And that I wasn't well. That it was natural for all of it to happen. That, after all, I had lost Eduarda. But that we weren't good for each other. That she had become aware of my unbalance. Everyone had. That the musicians were concerned about me. And that there were rumors that they wanted to remove me from the orchestra. 'Go see your doctor. This is very serious. You obviously need help.'

Marie's parents appeared, to offer support to their daughter. A line was drawn, them on one side, me on the other, three against one. They all looked at me the same way, as if I were an enemy, a foreigner. And that's what I was, in the final analysis. A non-Jew. I didn't have the slightest notion of what it means to arrive in Lod and see yourself surrounded by Jews, as Mira, Marie's grandmother, had once said. 'You get off the plane, look around, and see that there you're the majority. You don't have to explain anything to anybody. You're a Jew, and that's enough.' I didn't know what that was. Didn't have the least idea. I didn't speak their language. And they spoke together, saying the same thing, one complementing the other: 'Go away,' that's what they were saying. They talked about lawyers, the divorce process. Henri made it clear that Marie had absolutely no interest in anything. 'Financially, I mean.' It was just a question of talking it through and resolving everything.

I sat there, absorbing their threefold bombardment.

'What is it you want?' Marie shouted. 'Say it.'

I thought about saying that I wanted things to be different. And for her not to have betrayed me. And for Eduarda to be there, with us. I wanted to go back to conducting like before, without anguish, without fearing people, without doubting my knowledge, without depending on the score or the musicians' response.

'Say it. What is it you want? Tell me.'

'I want the names.'

'What names?'

'The names of the people you're involved with.'

The three of them stared at me, waiting for something more.

'Do something,' Monique told her husband in a low voice. 'Take a stand.'

Marie went upstairs, I followed her, and when she slammed the bedroom door in my face, I started screaming that I'd put a bullet in my head if she didn't come back to me.

Only then did I notice that Henri was at my elbow. 'Calm down,' he kept saying, over and over. I hate it when people ask me to calm down; it makes me even more exasperated. I explained this to him as we descended the stairs.

In the living room, Henri and I sat down, neither of us speaking. I was perspiring a lot, and my blood pressure must have gone down. They served me something to drink, lemonade, very sweet.

'Are you all right?' Henri asked.

'I need to eat something,' I replied. I hadn't put anything in my stomach since the morning before, and I felt weak.

We went to the kitchen, where Henri gestured to the help that we wanted to be alone. He himself got some smoked salmon, cheese, and bread. 'Try this olive oil,' he said. I ate without appetite, not tasting anything. I chewed and swallowed, thinking about what Marie had said. Henri talked nonstop. He put other types of olive oil on the table; 'This one has basil.' I was impressed by how long he'd managed to keep up a one-way conversation about nothing. 'And this one is flavored with garlic and honey. What an incredible city São Paulo is, don't you agree? In the old days, when I traveled, I'd go to Fauchon and think that we'd never have anything like that here. Did you know that Monique would bring back this pâté, the Barilla, in her suitcase? We didn't have anything here in Brazil. Today, when I travel nothing surprises me. In terms of power, wealth, luxury, or poverty. We have it all here, in my view, as good or better.'

After a time, he said he was worried about me. 'I'm very fond of you.'

'Please,' he said after a long pause, 'I know you can understand my situation as a father. I'm making a sincere request. Leave my daughter alone.'

'I can't,' I replied. And left.

When I got to the hotel they informed me that someone was waiting for me in the library. I went there, and an older man stood up when he saw me. His clothes shabby, his hair white, his skin sunburned. He identified himself as the driver who had run over my daughter.

I felt as if everything were repeating itself. It was as if at that moment I were again being notified of Eduarda's death.

'The dog is still alive,' he said.

He told me that he had tried to help Eduarda, that she had simply stepped in front of the bus, that he guessed the dog had been to blame, because he couldn't understand how she could step out onto such a busy street. He also told me how insensitive the onlookers had been, how they had watched it all and done nothing, how he'd had to scream for help. He said he'd stayed at the morgue until two a.m., and that there wasn't anything to identify the girl, nothing, not a scrap of paper. And that he eventually went home, taking the injured dog. The dog had been incredibly lucky: the bus driver's son-in-law worked as a watchman in a veterinarian's office, and that's why its life had been saved.

'He's at my house now,' he said. 'He limps and has to be fed by hand, but he's all right.'

He had decided to look for me because he thought I might want my daughter's dog. He could bring it to me if I wished.

We looked at each other; actually, both of us looked at nothing. He told me he had a daughter two years older than

Eduarda. I had the impression that somewhere nearby, Villa-Lobos's *Waltz of Sorrow* was playing.

'Do you hear that music?' I asked.

'What music?'

We said goodbye. As he was leaving, I asked for his address.

That night, when I went onstage, I was greeted with applause. I had fought with my assistant, who was waiting for me at the dressing room door to ask if I was sure I didn't want the scores. 'I don't like people to talk to me before concerts, it distracts me. You should know that by now.'

'I'm following the new orchestra manager's orders.'

That was precisely what irritated me. I didn't even know there *was* a new manager. Who had hired him? 'I give the orders here,' I said.

'We just thought you might like to have the score,' she answered. 'That's all.'

'A different maestro,' I said, 'would let you go right now.'

There are many names for what happened there that night. But all I can say is that I was abandoned by the music. It was clearly a punishment. The music had punished me by hurling me into the void. Inside me something was saying, There's nothing more for you. It's over. Enough. Go away. It escaped me completely, not just a phrase but the music in its entirety. It did no good for the concertmaster to save me at the mistaken entrance. I lost the music. And when the whole orchestra was about to crash before my eyes, a cell phone rang in the audience.

I stopped the orchestra. The phone continued to ring, and a murmur ran through the hall. It was the opportunity for salvation. In the wings was my assistant, with the scores in her hands. All I had to do was signal. And then restart

Camargo Guarnieri's *Uirapuru*, which I had practically dismembered, from the top. Now, it was just a matter of beginning again, confidently. With concentration. A very simple thing, actually. It was just a question of moving on. I don't know what happened to me. I felt an immense nothingness around me. I looked at the musicians, at the audience. None of it had the slightest significance anymore. Not without Eduarda. Without Marie.

I turned my back on the orchestra and walked off the stage.

24

'MAESTRO,' I HEARD SOMEONE call me. 'How are you?' I asked when I saw the woman approach the table in the restaurant where I was having lunch. Besides fans, it was only doctors with whom I was that receptive, though I hated both to the same degree. There are few things in the world worse than doctors. You're dying, and either they go on killing you or they don't let you die. They shove tubes down your throat, open your belly, hook your heart up to a machine and keep you alive. Or they kill you, through the same procedure. That's why, fearing they'd give me some terrible news, I treated them as though they warranted respect. It was as if that way I could avoid a diagnosis of cancer or some other incurable disease. With admirers who came up to praise me, I also experienced the sensation that I had to respect them or the music would punish me, by taking something away from me. There was no longer any reason to act that way with the fans. But my attitude was mechanical, a habit.

She's going to greet me, say she loves my concerts, I thought. That I'm a great conductor of Strauss. It was what they always said. 'How are you, maestro?' the lady asked, giving off the odor of age, old clothes, old perfume, old powder. I remembered that it was the same smell that my grandmother used to emanate. 'I almost didn't recognize you,' she said. 'My husband said: "Yes, it's him." And I thought: No, no, it can't be.'

I smiled.

'You've put on a little weight,' she continued.

Trying to be amiable, waiting to hear a compliment, and that's all I got. Serves me right for being polite, I thought.

I left the restaurant, not knowing what to do with the rest of the afternoon. It was a strange feeling, not working. Not studying, not rehearsing, not conducting, not wearing myself out every day. I had canceled all my concerts outside Brazil for the year. 'You mustn't do that,' my agent had said. 'At least conduct in London.' He didn't have the faintest idea of how relieved I felt at not having to step onto the podium. Musicians in any orchestra in the world know whether a conductor is good or bad in the first few minutes of the rehearsal. Even before the rehearsal, just by the way he comes into the room, just by the way he greets you. They're always ready to love you or to fuck you. It was very good to be free of that feeling. I no longer even had my orchestra. The newspapers gave my departure a lot of space. 'How are you going to live without the orchestra?' one journalist asked. 'By living,' I replied. 'But what about your public?' You'd think I was Julio Iglesias. Fuck the public, I thought. Everyone expressed surprise. I had surprised myself. I always ended my contracts with orchestras in horrible fights. It was the first time I had simply turned my back and walked away.

I got in the car I had recently rented; the driver was listening to the radio.

'You can turn that off, please.'

'Where to, maestro?'

I looked at my appointment book. *Alameda Itu, 1432* was written there. Why had Marie gone to that location? I leafed through the previous pages, consulting the information for the last ten days in which I had followed her around the city.

September 19 – Home of her cousin Muriel, acupuncturist; lunch on Oscar Freire with unidentified woman. Oscar Freire, no destination. Enters and leaves stores. Remainder of day at home.

September 20 – Receives visit from a couple (???). Chocolate shop, two packages for gift. Lingerie store. Marie was a shopper, like her mother. Expensive clothes, expensive designer shoes, always. Everything quite simple but quite expensive. And no ostentation, because the refined rich aren't ostentatious. The refined rich, as a conductor friend used to say, wear brown with black. And the tacky rich, brown with beige. *Uses cell phone at traffic light (12:25) – With whom? Pamplona, Marie on the phone. Marie at her father's office. Marie at the pharmacy. Marie at tennis lesson. Instructor suspicious. Check everything.*

I didn't always understand my own observations. I checked some more notes and went back to those for that day: *Itu, 1432.* That's where I had lost Marie that morning; *11 o'clock, entrance to the building* was jotted down. I must have dozed off for half an hour, I thought. I remember that when I looked at my watch, before lunch, it was one o'clock. It took no more than fifteen minutes for me to get to the restaurant. Therefore Marie left the building between 11:15 and 11:45. Where could she have gone?

'Did you see when the lady got into the car?' I asked the driver.

He'd already told me several times that he hadn't seen Marie leave; he'd been distracted, reading the sports section. But I couldn't help repeating the same question. This last time, I wrote down the answer: *Was reading newspaper.* You can be a good liar if you have a good memory, I'd learned that many years ago. That's how I discovered everybody's lies. By always checking.

I thought about going back to Marie's house, but with every passing day it was becoming harder for me to approach the place. The security guards grew suspicious whenever my car parked in the vicinity, and I had to watch from a distance, hiding behind an ancient mango tree not far from the residence.

'Where to, sir?' asked the driver.

I didn't want to go back to that square. Its smell of disinfectant bothered me. Every day the rich people on that street would send someone to clean the square. They were constantly disinfecting the square, fearing their children would catch some disease. But they didn't stop taking their dogs to shit there; in fact, they weren't even disgusted by the feces of their own dogs. It's the feces of the neighbor's dog that generates infections, they thought. And so they disinfected the square. I had several times seen the gardener from one of the mansions throw creosol there. They even threw creosol on the benches. Really, I prefer Iraq. Every time I see those houses, those people, those gardens, those nannies, I think that. Much better, Iraq.

'Shall we go back to the hotel?' the driver asked.

That was something I liked to do, take Versed and sleep all afternoon.

That afternoon, however, I don't know why, I felt like visiting Adriana. She received me coldly, but after a few minutes we were chatting amicably. She told me she'd stopped drinking and gone back to Alcoholics Anonymous. 'I feel very good there. I don't know just how it works, but the fact is it *does* work. You hear a bunch of people telling a bunch of stories, so much bad stuff, so many gutters, so much fighting, so much divorce, so much repentance, so much abuse, so much crap, that it gets to you. I leave there determined not to drink that day. It's a minimal victory, you don't even think about never drinking again. All you have to take care of is today. Today I didn't drink, that's what you have to say.'

It was unpleasant to hear her say she'd started drinking again because of me. And that she'd 'truly' fallen in love with me. And that she'd suffered greatly because of our breakup.

'I like you,' was all I could bring myself to say. And I regretted that, because it had very unpleasant consequences. We ended up in bed, and I couldn't get it up.

'It's normal,' Adriana said. 'Who doesn't go limp once in a while?'

Adriana made me promise to call, and I promised, knowing I wouldn't do it. I never keep my promises.

I was at the square by eight a.m. the next day. I didn't want to risk missing Marie. 'Keep an eye out,' I told the driver, but the guy wasn't at all reliable. I could see that he was constantly distracted. The moment some nanny appeared, he would drop everything. That morning's nanny was horrible, fat as an armoire, and even so he was excited. The truth is that a woman can be ugly, trash, have a huge ass, hairy legs, a face like a monkey, rotten teeth, and there's always some man willing to screw her. Always.

I got distracted too.

'I just came to warn you,' said the security man from Marie's house, who popped up in front of me, taking me by surprise. 'The boss said he's calling the police if you stay here.'

'Oh?' I said, taking out my wallet. Parking valets, watchmen, doormen, all those guys work a lot better if you offer them a tip. I gave him some money.

'Say I disappeared,' I told the young man.

'Right. But it won't do any good for you to come back.'

'Really?'

'The lady left last night.'

'For where?'

'I don't know. Overseas.'

I took out my wallet again and gave him a hundred. 'It shouldn't be hard to find out where.'

'I'll try,' he answered, accepting the bill.

The day hadn't even begun and I had nothing to do. Absolutely nothing.

I stuck my hand in my pocket and got the piece of paper that had been there for weeks. I had crumpled it several times to throw it away, but it was still there, in my pocket.

'Do you know how to get to Vila Clementino?' I asked.

'I live there, sir.'

I asked him to take me there. 'To this address,' I said, handing him the paper on which I had written the address of the driver who had run over my daughter.

It doesn't even look like Eduarda's dog, I thought when the lady of the house took me to the concreted backyard where he slept.

'What's his name?' the woman asked.

From the kitchen came the smell of freshly cooked beans. I felt like eating. 'Tatu,' I answered, lying. I couldn't remember the dog's name.

'We didn't know. We called him Roque. My son came up with it.'

'Roque, Roque,' I called out. The dog rose with difficulty and limped toward me. He was thin, weak, but even so he managed to wag his tail.

'He recognizes you,' the woman said. 'He's like you see

him, in bad shape, the poor thing. I crumble up his food and feed him by hand. Sometimes he vomits it all up. The vet told us to give him milk, but you know, it's not every day we can do that.'

We stood there for a few moments, while I patted Roque's head. The telephone rang, the woman excused herself. I liked the place, I don't know why, but I felt good there. The living room, the kitchen we had come through to get to the backyard, a silent spot, cool, and everything gave off a nice smell of cleanliness, of soap and water.

When she returned, I had made up my mind. 'I'm taking the dog,' I said.

I was on my way out when the woman asked if I wanted to have lunch. I was starving and so I accepted.

25

I SUCKED UP THE MILK with the syringe and placed it in Roque's mouth. He drank a little over six ounces altogether. He seemed more lively, there on my side of the bed. I had taken him to the veterinarian the day before for tests and x-rays. Roque had suffered several fractures and the resulting calcification had compromised his joints. Surgery was needed to correct these problems, but was definitely not worth the trouble. 'A lot of suffering,' the vet said. He explained that the dog vomited because of the intense pain in his spinal column and that analgesics would help. I liked the veterinarian, Paulo, a polite young man who displayed compassion as he treated Roque. I thought that my daughter's dog was lucky after all, lucky not to need doctors. In their hands he would be intubated, cut up, stitched and later buried.

The night was martyrdom. Roque woke up several times, in pain. I gave him more medicine, and he had no sooner swallowed the analgesic before he was vomiting everything, in gushes. I called the reception desk for help, and Dorival, from room service, came with a chambermaid. While the sheets were being changed, we took Roque to the bathroom, cleaned him, and put him back on my bed, on a fresh towel. I got some oil from the closet and massaged his rear paws, just as the vet had showed me. Dorival mixed the analgesic with milk and used an eyedropper to keep Roque from vomiting again. It worked; the dog went to sleep and spent the rest of the night peacefully.

Now and then he would open his eyes and, seeing me reading, wag his tail. He rested his head on my leg, calm. Eduarda was crazy about that animal. Thinking about that completely ruined my sleep. I paced around the bedroom, with a horrible sensation in my chest. I didn't want to think about her, or remember anything. But when I came to my senses, the photos that Eduarda had taken on our European trip were in my lap. This is what's left, I thought. Our pictures. She and I at the home of my good friend Piero, a stage manager, a fellow who possessed many fine attributes, young, polite, from a rich family, handsome, talented and a very good person. I had worked with him in Palermo for several months. 'I'll give you a hundred dollars for every shortcoming you find in Piero,' I'd told Eduarda. The three of us strolled through the city, and I felt that Piero, with his amusing stories, had managed to get my daughter interested in opera.

'Staging operas in Parma is always dangerous,' he had told Eduarda. 'When they call on me to go there, I immediately ask: Is it Verdi? If it is, I don't go. Verdi is from that area, from Busseto, and if you're born there you drink the composer in your nursing bottle. They know every comma of the libretto. They know the arias backwards and forwards. You can't imagine what they do to guest conductors who show up there. They come to blows over the first row in the theater, and not because of the view. What they want is to be close to the maestro in order to heckle him at will. They tap him on the shoulder and tell him he's wrong. "That's not the tempo – *cammina*, maestro." There are some conductors who know quite well how to deal with it. There is a famous anecdote about one who, unhappy with the tenor, turned to a signora in the audience – as he was conducting, mind you – and asked: "Do you like this tenor?" He didn't even wait for her to start complaining. "*A me fa cagare*," he said. And the audiences come down hard on the tenors, too. At one staging of *Aida*, the fellow didn't sing the first C, which is a tradition, although it's not in the original score. He was booed so loudly that, at the end, he came back onstage with the arrangement in his hand, in Radames costume and all, and said: "Look at the score, you ignoramuses, Verdi didn't write that C." And you know what the audience shouted back? "Verdi was wrong! Verdi was wrong!"' Piero recounted a series of comic episodes, and Eduarda laughed a lot. Later, when we were alone, she told me: 'You can give me the hundred bucks. I found a real defect in your friend.'

'What defect?' I asked.

'All the guy talks about is opera. He's a bore.'

It wasn't good for me to remember Eduarda. I took a Versed and blacked out.

I woke at ten in the morning, to the ringing of the phone. The person at the other end of the line was speaking in Spanish. 'Wrong number, señora.' They were always making mistakes at the hotel. The Americans spend millions on technology, sophisticated gadgets that do practically everything by themselves. And then we hire illiterates to operate them. 'What's the weather like today?' I asked the receptionist. 'Cloudy,' she replied.

I showered, shaved, and used the syringe to give milk to Roque. Dorival helped me carry him to the hotel's courtyard so he could get a little exercise. Roque strained his front paws and managed to walk a few yards, with difficulty.

Then he dragged his rear paws, as if they were dead weights. And finally he gave up, because of the pain. That was it. After a few steps he lay down, exhausted.

'That's very sad,' Dorival said. 'I'm all the time telling my wife: if someday I should be crippled, please put me out of my misery. Feed me rat poison, do anything. Why live if it's like that? Look at the poor thing. I see him and, I swear to God, feel like putting a bullet in his head. For his own good.'

We took the dog up to the bedroom.

By eleven I was back at the square again. It had rained overnight, the benches were wet, and there wasn't a child in sight. Only two old men, each with his nurse. They walked with more difficulty than Roque, leaning on their nurses, who didn't give a damn about them. The women were carrying on an animated conversation between themselves. 'He thinks I don't know,' I heard one of them say. I thought they might be talking about me and I tried to follow them, but the security guard from Marie's house appeared at once.

'The lady went abroad all right,' he said.

'I already know that.'

'To Israel.'

'And when does she return?'

'They're afraid of you. They even spoke to a big shot in the police. And we have to let them know if you come around here. They changed telephone numbers.'

I asked if he could find out more details about the trip. 'Hotel, things like that.'

'The cook's already suspicious of me. I don't know anything else.'

It didn't take me five minutes to decide. I knew where Marie had gone and what she was going to do. She had gone to meet him. Images of Marie embracing Sandorsky outside the academy in Tel Aviv immediately leapt into my mind. Sandorsky and his monkey face. I guessed that the two of them had been talking all the while. 'Come over here,' he'd said. 'I'll protect you.' A flurry of sensations overcame me – rage, insecurity, desire for revenge, and especially humiliation. They'd been together the whole time. From the beginning, he'd been there, between us, the old monkey.

I got to the hotel and looked for Marie's books, where there were various notes that proved the connection between the two. I might be able to use that in court, as evidence of adultery. I'd have to check with my attorney. I jotted in my notebook: *Contact lawyer*. Thinking that Marie could be arrested for adultery disturbed me deeply. There's nothing like revenge. That forgiveness business isn't my thing. I can even forgive, but never forget. I turned everything upside down, in search of the books; I knew I'd kept some of them. They were in the hotel storeroom, along with a pile of newspapers I'd brought from the apartment. I opened one of them. 'His knee moves inside his pants, to mark the beat of the sound of drums that can only be heard in the Africa that is his brain.' She hadn't underlined this, but she should have. Sandorsky, the monkey – it was only in those terms that I thought of the professor. 'Impropriety is the Jew's style'; she hadn't marked that either. Sandorsky had no scruples, going after a married woman, above all a young woman, much younger than him. And besides that he was married. It occurred to me that I had done the same thing with Marie, I also was married, I also was older than her, but with me it all seemed natural, while with Sandorsky it was abominable. 'God is readying a catastrophe for these soulless Jews. If someday there is a new chapter in the Bible, you will read that God sent a hundred million Arabs to destroy the people of Israel for their sins.' Nor was that underlined. Sandorsky had carefully instructed Marie well on what to underline. 'Once again, the Jewish people are at a crossroads. Because of Israel. Because of Israel and the way Israel puts all of us in danger.' Why hadn't she underlined that as well? Because Marie wanted to go to Israel and wanted to ignore the risks that trip entailed, and it was all the fault of Sandorsky, who made her believe that her place was there. Far from me. 'Israelis are targets of three attacks,' it said in the paper. Three. Eighteen dead and over 115 wounded. Marie had ignored all these risks to go to be with her monkey lover.

I had made up my mind. That very day I went to an airline office and bought a ticket to London.

In the afternoon, I got my things together. Then I called Rachel. 'I'm coming to visit you.'

'Bring something for us to eat, a cake, anything. I'll fix some tea.'

Roque was in pain when Dorival and I put him in the back seat of the car. I stopped at a bakery and bought chocolate cream puffs and a walnut torte, which Rachel loved. There were lots of students there, some the age of my daughter.

'So, you brought Nego with you?' Rachel asked when she opened the door and saw me with the dog.

'What Nego?'

'The dog,' she replied, making Roque comfortable on the floor.

'I didn't know his name was Nego.'

'Eduarda wanted Preto, I was the one who suggested Nego. Nego is better than Preto, I feel.'

I told Rachel about the bus driver. We remained silent for a time.

'For me it gets harder and harder to believe in God. Saving the dog, just think.'

'I'm leaving for London tonight. I wanted you to keep Nego until I get back.'

At that moment, Esther appeared in the living room. Her pregnancy was visible.

'He wants to leave the dog with me,' Rachel said.

Esther didn't seem to mind. In fact, she didn't seem to understand.

'She's like that now, worse than Nego. She drags herself around the house like a zombie, doesn't eat. When the phone rings, she dashes for it like a poisoned rat. It's the butcher, the car insurance guy, it's the washerwoman saying the clothes are ready. It's everybody, except the one she's waiting for. I think the child's father is the minister of finance. Think about it, that must have been why she was let go. In the United States she'd make a pile of money with that story. Publish a book. The minister would be raked over the coals by the media. He'd lose his position. But here in Brazil, the poor woman can't say anything. If she says something, the minister will gain kudos for being an irresistible stallion. Did you see how worn-out she looks? Why don't you take her to Israel? It'd do her a lot of good, I have some relatives there.'

'Do you want to go to Israel?' I asked Esther when she came into the kitchen.

'No,' she answered.

'Go, child. Go while you can still travel. Once the baby is born you won't have the freedom. I tell her, maestro: when a child is born, along with it is born something called guilt. You can't even read a newspaper without feeling guilty. You think you have to watch the baby twenty-four hours a day. And that's just what happens. The other day I read somewhere that the worry a mother has over her child is a biological disease. A maternal neurosis that ensures the child's survival. If you ask me, it must be true. Because we women practically kill ourselves for our children. And now they say it's all biological, it's all chemistry. Depression, sadness, it's all because of some chemical deficiency in our body. Not even love is real. You see, Esther? It only lasts three years, which is the amount of time the woman needs the man to have a baby and start taking care of the child on her own. You don't have the man anymore. So why suffer? That business of romantic love is all nonsense. Nothing that a good Rivotril won't cure. You hear, Esther?'

'Stop, mother. Please.'

After Esther left, Rachel continued. 'I tell her all that because the poor thing is always crying. It's too much. It's more than I can stand. If she'd take just one Rivotril she'd be all right, like the two of us. You and I suffer more, we've had worst things happen to us, and here we are. You don't know what it's like to watch your husband die of cancer. One day, in the middle of an attack of horrible pain, he said to me: "Rachel, do something." What could I do, besides call the doctor and ask him to authorize another dose of morphine? And here I am. Strong and firm. Like you. Your Eduarda didn't know what life is. One day she came down here and had lunch with me and then watched cartoons on TV. As big as she was, she was still just a child. She hadn't even begun to live.'

We embraced as I left. Rachel promised to take good care of the dog.

Everyone thinks that the conductor's biggest fear is losing his memory. That's true. But the conductor's terror is losing his luggage. Every time I travel, it's the same thing. I've lost suitcases in Paris, New York, Milan, in several places. Suitcases with important scores, schedules, documents. It traumatized me. For a long time I would only travel with carry-on luggage. I could never weigh them, because I knew they wouldn't let anyone board carrying so much weight. Here in Brazil it was easy, but in Brazil everything is easy. In Europe, however, at boarding they often separate me from my baggage. And in general a single bag wasn't sufficient, so I started carrying two. 'Aren't you worried about your back?' a flight attendant once asked me.

On that flight it was different. What is there that's so important in a suitcase? I thought. Nothing, I could lose everything and I'd just go to a store and buy undershorts, socks, all those things, and that would be that. Therefore I wasn't worried when, in London, it took forty-five minutes for my bag to appear. I had a six-hour wait for the connecting flight to Tel Aviv, which wasn't much time. If you're going to Israel you have to show up at the airport four hours before the flight, and the Israeli police take pains to see that everything is a barrel of laughs.

As soon as I checked in, I was directed to a counter at the side where employees interviewed me assiduously. 'Why are you so serious in the passport photo?' they asked. My passport was shown to other agents, and since I don't speak Hebrew, I didn't have a clue about what they were discussing.

The interview lasted exactly one hour, and afterwards I went through five more interrogation checkpoints.

When I boarded the plane, I saw the agent who had interviewed me. 'Are you ready, maestro?' he said.

'Yes,' I replied, without understanding the significance of the question. Maybe he wanted to know if I was ready to take a chance on the plane blowing up. I was ready for anything, even to kill if necessary.

I thought that the safety instructions might be different

on the flight. But it was the same patter as always, about lifejackets and inflatable slides. You have to be very optimistic to think you're going to survive in case of mechanical failure.

I finally arrived in Tel Aviv in late afternoon. From the airport to the seaside, the entire city is made up of white houses, like small Bauhaus-style crates. But the oceanfront is a tragedy. You feel as if you were at Guarujá, or some other enclave of middle-class condominiums.

On the way to the hotel, the taxi driver offered me 'Russian whores. The best whores in the world,' he said. 'You have to try them, they're nice and young and very pretty. They're a pretty people, those Russians. And the whores are real hot. I speak from personal experience.'

Marie wasn't staying at the Hilton. Or at any other five-star hotel in the city; I called them all. I also called cheaper hotels, but no Marie. She was surely staying at the home of some friend of Sandorsky's. I asked the reception desk to find his telephone number for me. 'It's not in the phone book,' they said.

All I could do was wait till the next morning, and then look for her at the academy of music.

At night I went for a walk near the hotel. Tel Aviv is a pretty city. I went to the Romanian market, downtown, which has a quasi-Art Deco architecture. On the other side, lots of stores, cafes, night clubs and whores. A euphoric city. Sixteen-year-olds in army uniform. They finish their military duties and head for the mall, carrying a machine gun. The tension didn't come from the young people and their weapons. Only the old people are circumspect and frightened. They cross the streets, not as if they were in a hurry, but as if they were fleeing from something. Burnt-out cars and rubble are part of the scene.

In a bar two blocks from the hotel I saw men talking excitedly and taking notes. The owner, after some preliminary questions, asked if I wanted to participate in the game.

'What game?' I inquired.

'It's a pool. You try to guess where the next attack will be and place your bet. You also win if you get the place wrong but the district right. Do you know Tel Aviv?'

Before midnight, I was back at the hotel. I stayed at the reception desk looking for newspapers to read. The political cartoons were unbelievable. Before leaving for work, a citizen hugged his family, in tears, prepared never to see them again. Another one showed waiters working in helmets. I lost the desire to read, and went up to the room. I lay down on the bed, not sleepy, and tried to practice a Buddhist exercise against suffering: Close your eyes and imagine the woman who's causing your suffering as a sack full of blood and manure, full of garbage and crap. It didn't work for me.

I gave up on the exercise and called Rachel, asking for news of Nego.

'He's fine,' she said. 'But he misses you.'

Now the dog loves me, I thought, not feeling the least comfort.

26

'I DIDN'T KNOW YOU were in town,' said Sandorsky when he saw me. We shook hands, which made me uneasy. Lately, I had avoided any type of physical contact. As soon as I had handled money or greeted someone, I would immediately clean my hands with antibacterial disinfectant, which promised to kill ninety-nine percent of the germs. The majority of illnesses are transmitted that way, people wipe their nose, or their ass, pick up bills full of tuberculosis bacilli, and then shake your hand. They act as if they were your friends when in reality all they're doing is infecting you. That morning, I had left the disinfectant at the hotel, which disturbed me.

'I've been hearing nothing but good things about your orchestra,' Sandorsky continued. We were in his room at the Tel Aviv academy. Minutes earlier, his secretary had interrupted a meeting to tell him of my sudden arrival. We hadn't seen each other in years, but Sandorsky treated me as if we were old friends.

'I liked the last CD you recorded very much,' he said.

If you want to get along with a conductor, flatter him. A conductor basically lives for such things. But I wasn't a conductor anymore, something Sandorsky wasn't aware of. His words had no effect at all.

I asked about the explosion that had occurred not far from there that morning. Sandorsky explained that it had been army activity. 'They destroyed some Palestinian homes. Our laws allow that.'

'We also kill a lot,' I said.

'What?'

'We possibly even kill more than you.'

And I went on saying things that came into my mind in a confused fashion, things I'd read somewhere, I said that human cruelty knew no limits, and that wars were necessary because without them we would have no way of giving vent to the violence we inherited from our ancestors. 'Genetic violence,' I said. I also said that the role of hatred, philosophically speaking, was to prevent the end of our species. 'None of that is my own thinking,' I explained. 'I read a lot.'

Sandorsky sat before me like a frightened monkey.

'You know why I've come here,' I said.

Outside, a student was practicing Saint-Saëns, which turned my stomach. I'd had it with Impressionist froth. Mahler, yes, because he knew how to cut to the bone. A thousand times better the stench of Mahler, I thought, the hard truth of Mahler.

'Marie,' I continued.

'How is she?' asked Sandorsky. 'I hear she has plans to go to the United States.'

No froth. The expressionists point out the world's stench, I thought. Straight from the hip. They open themselves up, show their insides. Their blood.

'If you really liked Marie, you'd advise her to go to Switzerland,' I said, finding it difficult to distance myself from the music.

'What are you talking about?'

I replied, when I finally managed to focus, that he, being Jewish, should take into account the rate of anti-Jewish incidents. 'In Switzerland it's at 0.5 persons per day, an index that experts consider low,' I said. 'That's where you'd take her if you really loved her.' I said there was no chance of peace in Israel, that there was territory to be returned and Sharon was an utter fool. That taxi drivers, besides offering me Russian prostitutes, told how they'd lost a friend, a son, a neighbor, a cousin. That they'd seen a bus, a building, a supermarket blow up. That I myself had seen several first-response teams around the city. And that I could smell burnt human flesh wherever I went. 'The slaughter will continue,' I said. Sandorsky tried to interrupt, but I didn't let him. I said he was going to die at any moment, and Marie as well. That the two of them could be in a restaurant and be engulfed by a fireball. 'Aren't you ashamed of hiding Marie?' I asked. 'Of exposing her to so much danger?'

Sandorsky looked at the door, as if calculating the fastest way to get there.

'I've come to get Marie,' I said.

'Frankly, I don't know what you're talking about.'

'She's here in Tel Aviv. In your house. And I'm willing to do anything to get her out of your claws.'

We argued a little before I called him a 'lying monkey', and Sandorsky demanded that I leave. When I refused, claiming my rights as Marie's husband, he exited, leaving me alone in the room. I stayed there for a good length of time, searching through drawers and looking for proof, until someone came to remove me. He was a musician, surely. A cellist with large hands, the balls of his fingers thick. I know that rabble. 'You can give up on your career,' I said. 'You'll never be anything.' I told him that one of my qualities as conductor was intuition, that I knew whether a musician had talent just by looking at him, which was an obvious lie. 'You're nothing. You have a disgusting look to you.' I said I knew several words in Yiddish. I explained I wasn't meshuga. 'But you are. If you think you're going to be a musician, that you're going to play in the Berlin Philharmonic, you're meshuga.' The young man began to laugh. 'You're a schmuck. A nobody.' My shouting attracted two more musicians, who grabbed me and led me to the street.

I knew exactly what to do to solve that problem.

I bought a new notebook, hired a car and driver, and spend the rest of the day waiting for Sandorsky in front of the academy. At 6:15 he left the locale and went home, to a neighborhood on the outskirts of Tel Aviv, where the rich live. I parked at the corner and observed my surroundings. It was as if the war didn't exist there. Imported cars, mansions, peace. Rich people are the same the world over. Indifferent to the pain of the world. Potbellied men and overly thin women. The truth is that, today, fat women are poor. Rich women are practically undernourished. Sandorsky's own wife, who arrived home not long after him, was one of those thin lettuce-eaters. For women like that, hunger is the enemy of perfection.

At 11:15, I gave up. I asked the driver to take me to the hotel. En route I asked if he could find me a Russian prostitute. He said yes, and he could get me more, 'two or three, if you like'.

I showered, got dressed, and was ordering food from room service when there was a knock on the door.

It was the Russian woman.

'Would you like some dinner?' I asked.

She didn't speak English. We ate in silence, and I thought about Marie. She definitely wasn't at Sandorsky's house; the monkey was married. She was staying at an apartment she'd rented for trysts. That's where they coupled, where Marie gave herself and betrayed me. There she spread her legs and engulfed him the way the Russian prostitute engulfed her clients. Horrible images of the two copulating came into my head so clearly that I completely lost my appetite.

She almost didn't eat anything either, my Russian, who wasn't pretty but had the freshness of youth. Every young woman, even if she's not pretty, has that type of beauty. To be eighteen, twenty, is in itself a kind of beauty.

After room service took away our table, the Russian woman lay on the bed and started removing her clothes.

'No,' I said.

I sat her on the sofa, turned on the television. We sat side by side, and that calmed me a little. I went into the bedroom and got the baton I had bought in New York, fiberglass 380 millimeters, by Pickboy.

'I'm a conductor,' I said. She took the baton and removed it from its plastic case.

'That's the best baton there is,' I continued. 'And light, you see? Look at the cork here on the end.'

She played with the baton, making various gestures. I felt ridiculous at that moment, trying to impress a Russian prostitute. I took the baton out of her hands and threw it in the trash. Then I got money from my wallet, handed it to the girl, and sent her away. It was late, and I needed to sleep.

I awoke the next morning to Rachel's phone call. Nego had died during the night. 'It was for the best,' she said. 'He was suffering a lot from the pain. And then he got hooked on analgesics and couldn't sleep; he was very agitated.'

I made no progress in the next couple of days. Only on Friday did things start to change. I was near the academy, waiting for Sandorsky to come out so I could follow him, when I heard someone call my name. It was a maestro from

Poland who had been guest conductor a few times for my former orchestra in Brazil.

He told me he'd just come from Buenos Aires, and had spent two days in São Paulo seeing old friends. And that he'd run into Marie at the Municipal Theater. 'I didn't know you two had separated,' he said.

At first I thought it was another of Sandorsky's tricks, that the monkey knew his movements were being carefully monitored, so he'd sent the Pole to throw me off the scent. I began asking a lot of questions, and the conductor, alarmed, started backpedaling, saying he wasn't really all that sure, that it might not have been Marie.

At the hotel I searched through my address book and found the number of the detective agency I'd contacted in São Paulo when I first became suspicious of Marie's behavior.

I called and hired their service. 'If you're quick, I'll pay double.'

I continued to follow Sandorsky, with no progress. There was always a strange coincidence: wherever I went, there would be bombings the next day. A restaurant where I'd eaten on Tuesday blew up. A pharmacy where I'd bought aspirin blew up. A supermarket where I'd bought bottled water blew up. I thought about the people in the pool; they must make a lot of money on that sordid pastime.

On Monday, the phone woke me up.

'This is Raul,' a voice said.

'Who?'

'The detective.'

He told me he'd found Marie. She had in fact never left the country. She was living on Rua Indianópolis, number 134, apartment 2. She went around with bodyguards.

I hung up the phone and thought about the security man who'd given me the information. The sonofabitch.

Before leaving for London, I went looking for Sandorsky again. He refused to see me, and I was forced to wait till he left the academy.

'I came to apologize,' I said as soon as he appeared.

He ignored me. He got in his car and left.

27

THERE WAS NOTHING TO do until it was time to board for São Paulo. So I decided to go to a land and naval weapons fair organized by the government of India. I'd read something about it on the plane and become interested. I caught a taxi and gave the driver the address. It was raining heavily in London, traffic wasn't moving, and the city seemed on the verge of collapse.

It took nearly an hour to get to the place. At the very first stand was a model smiling at the visitors, next to a very distinguished gentleman in a three-piece suit who was talking about the ease of use of an automatic rifle.

They spoke of the costs and benefits of specific arms, with thermal sensors, that needed no light to find the target.

'What can I do with this?' I asked an American vendor who was selling telescopic sights.

'Our contribution is the technical end. You come up with the idea. And with the money, of course.'

High-ranking officers of the Zimbabwean army were negotiating enthusiastically. India, Tanzania, there were people from everywhere, buying arms of every sort, and no one spoke of destruction, extermination, the end, but only technology, precision and efficiency.

'Man is a being for death.' Who was the author of that phrase?

I spent the entire afternoon wandering back and forth, analyzing every kind of weapon. Now and then I would go up to vendors and hear snippets of quite friendly conversations. Those wagers of war are very polite when it's time to settle on price. They sell not only weapons but an entire military paraphernalia, if you wish, and it's not the rich who buy. Actually, it's the rich who sell. The buyers are the poor countries, the poorest on the planet.

I was tired of looking at things. Before leaving Tel Aviv, we had run into hellish traffic because of yet another attack. A bus had blown up, killing nine people.

I saw an older woman being carried on a stretcher to an ambulance. She was wearing a blue blouse and had no shoe on her right foot. She gazed at me so intensely that I had the impression she was trying to tell me something important. I thought about getting out of the car.

'She's dead,' the driver said.

Walking among the stands, I could still picture the woman's expression.

It was 6:15 when I realized I hadn't eaten anything all day. I took a taxi back to the airport.

I changed my mind about getting something to eat; everything seemed repulsive.

I boarded at nine o'clock. I took a Versed and didn't wake up until the plane was landing in São Paulo.

'I want you to meet someone,' Adriana said when she opened the door. She was wearing a T-shirt and panties, her hair tousled as if she had just got out of bed.

I had arrived two days earlier and didn't know what to do. I couldn't get up the courage to go to the address on the piece of paper that had never left my pocket: Rua Indianópolis, number 134, apartment 2. I had already seen Raul, and I had all the information. Photos, reports, transcripts of wiretaps on the home of Marie's parents.

I had listened to various tapes, and the conversations were always the same: trivia, confidences, arguments, a lot of family nonsense. What caught my attention was the frequency with which the name David was mentioned. 'David's coming to get me', 'David is going with me', 'Bring David'. David had to be Marie's latest. The family had at last found someone with whom she could talk, as Maiakovskii would say, 'eyebrow to eyebrow'. A rich Jew, some diamond exporter, someone who, like her, understood perfectly the meaning of sentences like 'The extermination of the Jewish nation would not make Islam lose a single night's sleep, unless it were the night of the celebration', underlined in the books of her favorite authors.

It was also Raul who had sold me the gun that was now tucked inside my jacket. I didn't know why I'd bought it; every time I held it a chill ran down my spine and horrible images came into my mind. Facts, inconclusive evidence, I pondered it all, Marie, David, and thinking about those things in such a confused way paralyzed me. That's why I went to see Adriana. I thought she could help me, though I didn't know just how. Adriana, I thought, had been a secretary, she knew how to organize, and that was what I needed, order, method, an agenda. You have to call this one and that one, you've got a meeting with somebody or other. Pay this. Collect that. It was pleasant to arrive at my office and know that Adriana had taken care of me, and that all I had to do was function.

'This is Valéria,' said Adriana, leading a girl of no more than twenty by the hand. 'She's studying journalism and lives here now.'

'Hi, Valéria,' I said.

The girl had nothing to say, nor did I, but Adriana made sure there was no silence. She said she was working as an assistant for a film production company. 'We're going to film the life of Euclides da Cunha.'

I could just imagine what a piece of crap that would be.

Adriana ordered pizza, and the three of us ate in the kitchen, Valéria silent and Adriana relating stories about the new production. She was very impressed by the fact that Euclides would write on his cuffs when he had no paper. 'The most terrible thing of all is his son, Euclidinho, having the same name and dying the same way as his father. I think that's sensational, for the film. An incredible story, father and son killed by the same man, in the same way.'

When it was time to leave, Adriana walked me to the door.

'Do you like her?' she asked in the hallway by the elevator. 'We're together.'

'Who?'

'Valéria and me. I'm truly in love.'

The thought hadn't even occurred to me.

'I never thought it would be this good to get it on with a woman. When it comes to pleasure, it's the woman who knows about things. Come back one of these days and I'll tell you the whole story. Valéria is incredible.'

I left feeling terrible. I was happy to find Adriana well, but at the same time it was as if I had lost her forever.

I had nowhere else to go. The day before, I had visited Rachel. She and Esther were planning a stay in Rio de Janeiro. 'I'm taking this girl to get some fresh air. I haven't been to Rio in some time, but I have the recollection of that wide sidewalk by the ocean, the beach, it'll do the girl a lot of good. You know, maestro, I'm doing what a mother should do: taking care of her daughter. Just think, I almost didn't have a daughter, and today I have one who needs me, and on top of that, I'm going to be a grandmother. I must say, that completes me. It changed my life. I almost don't remember anymore my old man dying of cancer. Now I only think about the baby.'

Rachel wasn't the same. She barely looked at me during the visit. She had refused to talk about my dog. 'He died, that's all there is to it. I'm not going to make you suffer by listening to the details.' She moved back and forth, putting clothes into suitcases and giving orders to Esther, who also wasn't the same. She listened to her mother attentively, felt protected, resigned. And she was pretty. Pregnancy had given her a gentleness.

'We told the minister to go to hell,' Rachel confided.

'What minister?'

'The minister who's the father. The baby's father, have you forgotten?'

I asked for details of the story.

'Some other time, when Esther's not around,' Rachel said. 'I will say this one thing: There's nothing better in life than telling a cabinet minister to go to hell. I felt a sense of accomplishment, a warmth in the heart. I even repeat it to myself: "Go to hell, Mr. Minister."'

That afternoon, I thought about going back to Rachel's house. But there was something to be done, I knew. I wandered aimlessly for some time before deciding. Actually, the decision had been made some days earlier, but I was trying to postpone it, as if by postponing, something would happen to turn things around.

I took a taxi to Marie's new address. A building with a tiny square in front, on a small, brick-lined dead-end street. That was where she lived, a small villa, a rustic spot. It didn't even seem like São Paulo.

Because of the rain no one was in the square. The lights on the second floor were off. I hummed *Waltz of Sorrow*. Since arriving back in Brazil, I couldn't get that piece of music out of my head. I sat on a bench and waited. I reread several times the letter Teresa had sent me at the hotel. She said she was well and apologized for the way she had treated me. Further: she said she didn't hold me responsible for what had happened to our daughter. She also spoke of her new life with Cláudio. She was happy, Fort Worth was a pleasant place. Cláudio was satisfied with his job. 'We're adopting a baby,' she said at the end.

I put the letter in my pocket and went on waiting. I don't know how much time went by. It was almost eight p.m. when Marie entered the garage. I recognized her immediately. Her hair in a bun on top of her head. I felt a surge of energy course through me. A few minutes later, the lights in the apartment went on.

I got up, paced from side to side, not knowing what to do. I stuck my hand in my jacket and felt the gun cold against my fingers. I thought about Marie. About Eduarda. About Roque. About my orchestra, about music. Everything had come to an end, finally. Dried up. It was no longer possible to return to the hotel, no longer possible to go on. Nor to stay, to stop, to move.

SPECIAL THANKS

To Rubem Fonseca, *'il miglior fabbro'*

To Luiz Schwarcz, editor and dear friend

To Arnaldo Cohen, for valued information

To Roberto Minczuk, for the music lessons

A NOTE ON THE AUTHOR

Patrícia Melo is a novelist, scriptwriter and playwright. Her novels *The Killer*, *In Praise of Lies* and *Inferno* are all published by Bloomsbury. In 1999, *Time* magazine included her among the fifty 'Latin American Leaders for the New Millennium'.

A NOTE ON THE TRANSLATOR

Clifford E. Landers has translated from Brazilian Portuguese novels by such writers as Rubem Fonseca, Jorge Amado, João Ubaldo Ribeiro, Jô Soares, Chico Buarque, and José de Alencar as well as shorter fiction by Lima Barreto, Rachel de Queiroz, Osman Lins, and Moacyr Scliar. He received the Mario Ferreira Award in 1999 and a translation grant from the National Endowment for the Arts in 2004. His *Literary Translation: A Practical Guide* was published by Multilingual Matters Ltd in 2001.

A NOTE ON THE TYPE

The text of this book is set in Linotype Janson. The original types were cut in about 1690 by Nicholas Kis, a Hungarian working in Amsterdam. The face was misnamed after Anton Janson, a Dutchman who worked at the Ehrhardt Foundry in Leipzig, where the original Kis types were kept in the early eighteenth century. Monotype Ehrhardt is based on Janson. The original matrices survived in Germany and were acquired in 1919 by the Stempel Foundry. Hermann Zapf used these originals to redesign some of the weights and sizes for Stempel. This Linotype version was designed to follow the original types under the direction of C. H. Griffith.

by the same author

INFERNO Patrícia Melo £6.99 0-7475-6159-1

'A gritty, exciting and sometimes harrowing tale of life on the mean streets of Rio de Janeiro' ***Independent***

'As fast-paced and action-packed as a Tarantino film ... A classic story of breaking the vicious circle of crime' ***Scotsman***

THE KILLER Patrícia Melo £6.99 0-7475-3524-8

'Melo's success in creating a voice that renders Máiquel repellent yet intriguing, convincingly brutal yet residually sympathetic, makes *The Killer* a gruesomely readable novel' ***Times Literary Supplement***

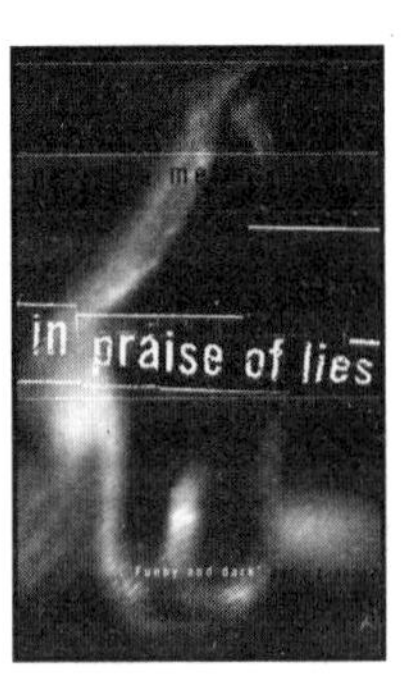

IN PRAISE OF LIES Patrícia Melo £6.99 0-7475-4573-1

'An enjoyable tongue-in-cheek thriller, Melo's story of how to commit the perfect murder is as refreshing for its exotic setting as for its professionally depressed hero, the lugubrious José Guber' ***Independent***

To order from Bookpost PO Box 29 Douglas Isle of Man IM99 1BQ www.bookpost.co.uk
email: bookshop@enterprise.net fax: 01624 837033 tel: 01624 836000

bloomsburypbks

www bloomsbury com/patríciamelo